"Why did you run away?" Jareth asked

Sophia glared at him. "You're th... ...e who's running away, not ... ...g to join David to be m...

His blue e... ...seemed to ... told your pa... ...is marriage," h... ...y all the secrecy, Soph... ...e not ashamed of David, are you?

She gasped out loud. "Of course not! He's the kindest, most decent man I've ever met."

"But a little dull?"

"You're hateful!" she snapped.

He remained cool. "You're running off to marry David to escape, because life at home got just too suffocating for you."

"You make it sound as if I'm using David," she accused.

"Well, aren't you?"

Joanna Mansell finds writing hard work but very addictive. When she's not bashing away at her typewriter, she's usually got her nose buried in a book. She also loves gardening and daydreaming, two pastimes that go together remarkably well. The ambition of this Essex-born author is to write books that people will enjoy reading.

Books by Joanna Mansell

HARLEQUIN ROMANCE
2836—THE NIGHT IS DARK

Don't miss any of our special offers. Write to us at the following address for information on our newest releases.

Harlequin Reader Service
901 Fuhrmann Blvd., P.O. Box 1397, Buffalo, NY 14240
Canadian address: P.O. Box 603,
Fort Erie, Ont. L2A 5X3

Sleeping Tiger
Joanna Mansell

Harlequin Books

TORONTO • NEW YORK • LONDON
AMSTERDAM • PARIS • SYDNEY • HAMBURG
STOCKHOLM • ATHENS • TOKYO • MILAN

Original hardcover edition published in 1986
by Mills & Boon Limited

ISBN 0-373-02866-0

Harlequin Romance first edition October 1987

CHAPTER ONE

SOPHIE couldn't remember feeling more ill in her entire life. Her body burned fiercely and ached relentlessly, while the throbbing pain in her head made her want to cry in sheer misery.

Woozily, she realised that she was no longer having to endure the bone-jarring gait of the camel. She was lying on the sand now, the cold chill of the ground seeping right through the thick blanket which covered her, making her shiver despite the feverish heat of her body. At night, the heat of the desert gave way to intense cold, and she huddled deeper inside the blanket as goose-pimples raced over her hot skin.

Vague memories of the past few hours drifted through her confused mind. She'd been travelling with a group of camel-herders, and she remembered the worry, the near-panic on their faces as the fever had taken a deeper grip on her, flushing her skin with its heat and soaking her hair with sweat. Then, a couple of hours after darkness had fallen two of them had come over and bundled her into a thick blanket, then somehow they had got her on to one of the camels.

Confused and frightened, she had tried to ask them what they were doing, where they were taking her, but she hadn't been able to remember a single word of her limited Arabic vocabulary. All that had come out were a few slurred, disjointed sentences in English. Even if the camel-herders had been listening to her, they wouldn't have understood a word she'd said. They hadn't been paying any attention to her, though. Instead, they had

seemed intent on taking her somewhere—but where?
And what would happen to her when they got there?

A little grimly, she realised she was about to find out.
Through the pounding in her head, she could hear
voices now.

'*As salaam alaykum.*'

That was Osman, the oldest of the camel-herders,
giving the formal Arabic greeting which she had heard
so many times since her arrival in the desert. 'Peace be
with you'. Then she heard a second voice, a voice she
didn't recognise, returning the greeting. '*Alaykum
salaam.*'

A swift flood of Arabic followed almost instantly.
They spoke so quickly, though, that she couldn't follow
what they were saying. Weakly, she tried to move; she
knew that she somehow had to find out what was going
on. The fever seemed to have done something strange to
her body, though, her arms and legs wouldn't move, and
all her bones seemed to have turned to jelly. Opening
her eyes briefly, she quickly shut them again as the
brilliant stars overhead whirled around in dizzy circles,
making her feel as if the entire world were doing some
crazy dance.

Panic was setting in now. Who was the stranger
Osman was talking to? All the old tales about white
slave-traders flitted through her pounding head, her
already soaked body broke out in a fresh wave of sweat.
Was Osman *selling* her?

That was nonsense, she told herself tremulously, such
things just didn't happen any more. Yet she was shaking
from head to foot, she knew she had to get away from
here, she just had to. If only she didn't feel so terribly
weak and ill——

With an enormous effort she somehow managed to
raise her head, but great waves of blackness instantly

rolled over her; the voices were fading away now, there was nothing except the fierce heat that burned inside her, the awful pain in her head, and the darkness, the endless darkness——

With a small sigh, Sophie collapsed back on the sand and slid into complete unconsciousness, which later in the night gave way to a deep, dreamless sleep.

When she finally woke up again, she didn't bother to open her eyes straightaway. In fact, she wasn't even sure that she *could* open them, they felt as if they were weighed down with rocks, and oh, her head ached so badly! The last twenty-four hours were little more than a blur in her confused memory; she remembered feeling feverish and funny, sort of hot and shivery at the same time, like a bad attack of 'flu. Only that wasn't possible, she reasoned—you couldn't catch 'flu in the desert—could you?

An enormous yawn engulfed her, then another. Lord, she was so sleepy! Then something else dawned on her, something rather alarming. It was so *quiet*. She'd got used to waking to the sounds of grunting and groaning from the camels against a background of colourful Arabic oaths as the camp erupted into activity. It had never been silent like this, she could almost feel the emptiness all around her. The camel-herders with whom she'd been travelling must have gone, they'd abandoned her out here in the desert!

Panic gripped her, she was afraid to open her eyes and have to face the truth. Yet in the end she somehow forced her heavy eyelids open and she peered around fearfully, while her heart started to beat a wild abandoned rhythm in her aching chest.

The landscape was very familiar, golden sun-drenched plains broken by chains of ochre rock, the only vegetation a sparse, coarse grass and tangled thorn bushes. Overhead, the vast expanse of bright blue sky was broken only by a thin line of clouds in the distance hovering over the shimmering outline of distant mountains. It was a desolation that could be frighteningly bleak or awesomely beautiful, depending on your point of view.

And it was empty. No herd of camels, no men bustling around noisily. Sophie swallowed convulsively, turned her head away from that terrifying emptiness— and then she saw him.

He was sitting just a few yards away from her, his face slightly turned away so that she had a chance to study him during these first few seconds without him being aware of it. He was wearing an *araagi*, the long Arab shirt of coarse white material, and underneath it loose cotton trousers, yet not the '*imma*, the long strip of cloth which most Arabs wore wound round the head. Yet from the dark, shaggy hair, the deeply tanned skin, the fierce aquiline features, she had no doubt that he was an Arab. Something inside her quivered, and quite suddenly her head cleared and blurred memories from last night slid back into her mind. She remembered the jolting ride across the desert, the stranger's voice she had heard talking to Osman. Was this the man Osman had been speaking to? Her eyes grew huge with fright. Why had she been left here? What did he intend to do with her? And who *was* he? A bandit? She'd been warned about bandits in this area, but she'd simply taken no notice. Blithely confident, she had enthusiastically launched herself into this great adventure, but suddenly it was falling to pieces all around her and she was scared to death.

Although she had been lying very still, rigid with fright, she must have made some small sound, some tiny movement, that alerted him to the fact that she was awake. A second later, he turned his head and a wave of pure shock thumped through her as she saw his eyes. Bright blue, the gorgeously brilliant colour of the gentians that her mother loved to grow in her rockery garden back home.

Not an Arab, then. No Arab had eyes like that. A million questions began to whizz around inside Sophie's head, but she didn't ask any of them, instead she just lay there and stared up at him.

'So,' he said, gazing back at her in a chillingly remote manner, 'you're finally awake.'

That cool voice was unmistakably English. Sophie gave an enormous sigh of relief and felt her dry mouth and throat slowly become moist again. Quite suddenly she felt very much better and forgot how deathly scared she'd been only seconds ago.

'Heavens, you gave me a fright! I thought you were a bandit!' she babbled a little lightheadedly. 'I was just trying to work out if you were after my virtue or my money. Or perhaps both!'

He didn't smile. In fact, he didn't respond at all, except to become, if anything, even more withdrawn. Sophie felt the first pricklings of unease, but brightly forced herself to ignore them.

'I guess I was pretty lucky,' she prattled on. 'You're probably the only other English person wandering around in this part of the eastern Sahara, and yet we've managed to meet up with each other. What do you reckon the odds are on that?'

'I've no idea, and I'm certainly not interested,' came his curt reply. 'Anyway, there's nothing particularly miraculous about the fact that you're here. The desert Arabs always know when a *khawaja*—a foreigner—is passing through their territory. Those camel-herders must have been very relieved that they could leave you with someone of your own kind.'

The vivid blue eyes were still cold and remote, and Sophie began to consider the slightly worrying possibility that she wasn't exactly welcome here. Then, with her usual happy knack for pushing unpleasant thoughts to one side, she dismissed that silly idea and smiled at him brilliantly—the same smile that, over the years, had reduced vast numbers of strong men to quivering wrecks. At the same time, she hoped she wasn't looking too much of a mess. She'd discovered long ago that, unfair though it was, being spectacularly pretty helped to solve an awful lot of life's problems. Although not in the least vain, she knew perfectly well that she rarely looked less than gorgeous. And when she tried hard, the effect was usually downright stunning. Right now, though, she suspected that her appearance was distinctly below par. Desert travel didn't allow many opportunities for even basic beauty care, and the fever had left her hair limp, her skin horribly dry.

All the same, he should have been showing just a flicker of interest. After a moment's consideration, she looked straight at that dark, unfriendly face, gave a tiny flutter of her thick, sweeping lashes and let her velvet brown eyes gaze into his invitingly.

Nothing! Not a single spark of response, the tiniest sign that he'd even noticed she was female, with an abundant share of all the feminine assets.

A little piqued, Sophie sighed silently to herself. This was going to be even harder than she had thought. She'd realised now that she had been dumped by the camel-herders, which meant that she was going to have to find someone else to take her to her final destination. This man looked as if he knew his way around—she was sure he was quite at home in the desert. Added to that, he spoke Arabic, which meant he would be perfect as a guide. The only trouble was, he was showing absolutely no inclination to be helpful.

Still, she'd keep trying, she decided with a fresh rush of determined optimism. After being an ugly duckling all her childhood, she had bloomed unexpectedly and quite spectacularly during late adolescence, and since then there hadn't been many men she hadn't been able to twine around her elegant little finger. In fact, come to think of it, there hadn't been any. So there wasn't any reason why her bandit-like rescuer should turn out to be an exception.

One step at a time, though, Sophie, she cautioned herself. This wasn't a man who would let himself be pushed into anything; he'd have to be very gently led, so that he didn't even realise he was doing exactly what she wanted him to do.

'I suppose we ought to introduce ourselves,' she suggested, giving him her warmest smile.

'No need for that,' he told her indifferently. 'I went through your belongings last night and found your passport. I know exactly who you are, Lady Sophia Carlton.'

'You went through my things?' she squeaked indignantly, sitting up sharply. Then she grabbed her head. 'Oh,' she moaned, 'I feel rotten, really dizzy, and my head hurts!'

'Then lie down and stop getting so over-excited,' he answered unsympathetically.

When the world had stopped whirling round and round in giddy circles, she threw a half-hearted glare at him.

'I bet you'd get a little excited if someone went through your things behind your back,' she accused.

He merely shrugged.

'It seemed a good idea to find out who you were. After all, you were dumped on me like a piece of unwanted luggage.'

'That was hardly my fault,' she insisted weakly. 'I paid those camel-herders to take me to Hajjar. The trouble was, they got panicky after I went down with that fever. I suppose they were scared they'd get into trouble if anything happened to me.'

'More likely they were worried about their camels,' he replied calmly. 'They couldn't afford to wait around for days until you got better, those camels needed water and the nearest wells are some distance away.'

Sophie stared at his infuriatingly impassive face.

'You sound as if you've got more sympathy for those camel-herders than you have for me,' she muttered a trifle sulkily.

'And why not?' came his smooth reply. 'These people have a hard enough life as it is, they don't need to be burdened with some spoilt little society brat who thinks it's fun to have a holiday somewhere different this year, away from all the usual tourist high spots. I'm sure it'll be the talk of your set, how Lady Sophia Carlton trekked through the Eastern Sahara in the company of all those colourful natives, enduring hardship and discomfort, but being so *brave* and coming out of it all with a gallant smile—not to mention a heap of photos to bore everyone to death with when you're finally back home again.'

The sarcasm that edged those cool tones was suddenly almost too much to take, especially in her present weakened condition. For a moment her velvet brown eyes revealed an unexpected vulnerability, a softness which she usually managed to keep well hidden under a sophisticated façade. Instinctively, she closed her eyes to shield her privacy. This man wasn't going to burrow under her skin, probe all her weaknesses, she vowed with an intensity that surprised her. Quite deliberately, she kept her eyes shut until she was sure she had her reactions under control again. Then she opened them and stared at him with a coolness which matched his own.

'Since you know who I am, perhaps you should return the compliment,' she said with rigid politeness.

He inclined his dark head.

'Jareth Kingsley,' he stated. 'No title, I'm afraid,' he added with deliberate derision, 'but I happen to believe that such honours should be earned, not inherited.'

I *won't* let him goad me, Sophie muttered to herself over and over, tightly clenching her small fists. It was so hard, though, there was something about this man that made all her hackles rise.

'Well, Mr Kingsley,' she got out at last with that same formal courtesy, 'I have a proposition to put to you.'

One near-black eyebrow lifted in a gently mocking gesture.

'This could turn out to be an interesting experience. I've never been propositioned by a Lady before.'

It was too much, her self-control simply snapped and she glared at him with pure hatred.

'All these miles and miles of empty desert, and I've had the bad luck to be stuck with the rudest, most unpleasant man I've ever met!' she threw back at him shrewishly. 'Can't you even try to be friendly? After all, we're obviously going to have to spend a lot of time together.'

At that, the dark eyebrow shot even higher.

'We most certainly are not!' he retorted.

Sophie felt her bottom jaw abruptly fall. Was he just going to abandon her, then? Leave her here on her own, in the middle of this vast, arid wilderness? At the thought of it, she began to tremble, all the fight suddenly drained right out of her. Instead, she felt peculiarly weak, almost hollow, and stupid, stupid tears began to prickle at the back of her eyes. It was the fever, that was all, she was absolutely sure of it, but how humiliating to be reduced to this weepy, shaky state in front of this aggravatingly self-controlled stranger.

'But you can't mean——' she began, then hurriedly stopped. Oh damn, her voice was all quavery, if she couldn't get some kind of control over herself then he'd know exactly how scared, how vulnerable she was right now, and she just knew he'd take advantage of it. There was no warmth, no kindness in Jareth Kingsley; she should have seen that from the very beginning. Those remote blue eyes were so beautiful, almost too beautiful for that starkly male face with its strong, powerful features, but they were cold, utterly soulless, as if no one really existed behind that outer façade.

Despite the growing heat of the sun, she abruptly shivered. What made a man like that, drained all the life out of him? One thing was certain, she'd never find the nerve to actually ask him. All her instincts warned her that this was a man who would guard his private life, his private emotions with terrifying ferocity. She was already more than a little scared of him, she didn't intend to rub him up the wrong way even further by asking a lot of awkward questions.

Anyway, there was only one thought dominating her mind right now. What was he going to do with her?

'You can't just—just leave me here,' she stammered, scared to death that he'd calmly announce that he intended to do just that.

'No, I can't,' he agreed, to her enormous relief.

A little confidence slowly seeped back into her veins.

'Then you'll take me with you?'

He gave a dark frown, as if the prospect didn't particularly please him. Then his shoulders lifted in a resigned shrug.

'I promised the camel-herders that I'd take you to Umra—that's a village a few miles to the north of here. But that's as far as I'm taking you,' he warned. 'You'll have to make your own arrangements after that.'

Sophie's delicate brows drew together in an unexpectedly stubborn line.

'But I don't *want* to go to Umra!'

The blue eyes glittered ominously.

'I wasn't aware that you were being given a choice.'

'But you still haven't heard my proposition,' she persisted. 'You see, I want someone to take me to Hajjar. I'll never make it on my own, I'll only get hopelessly lost, and it might be days, even weeks before I can find some more camel-herders travelling in that direction. If you'll take me, I'll pay you well, money's no problem——' A shadow suddenly crossed her face. 'Unless those camel-herders stole my money,' she added a little disconsolately.

'Your money's perfectly safe. You were lucky, they were quite honest,' he told her. 'Not that it makes the slightest difference. I'm going to take you to Umra, and not a step further. If you've an ounce of sense inside that addled head of yours, you'll make your way straight back to England from Umra. There's absolutely nothing at Hajjar, it's a small town in the middle of nowhere. No doubt they'll be sorry to miss a visit by Lady Sophia Carlton, but I daresay they'll manage to get over the disappointment.'

'You really enjoy making nasty remarks, don't you?' she muttered resentfully. 'And with or without you, I'll get to Hajjar.'

He frowned irritably.

'Why?' he demanded. 'Just because you enjoy being contrary?'

'No,' she answered with some dignity. 'Because my fiancé, David Stanton, is there. Once I've joined him, we're going to be married.'

And to her satisfaction, that briefly silenced him. Not for long, though. He stared rather pointedly at her bare left hand, then flicked that cool blue gaze directly at her.

'You're not wearing an engagement ring,' he observed.

'David and I don't need any symbols of our love,' she pronounced rather haughtily.

As those blue eyes continued to hold her in their relentless gaze, Sophie fervently hoped that he wouldn't ask too many difficult questions. Not that she was worried about giving the answers, of course she wasn't, it was just that she didn't want to talk about David to this man. He'd be quite incapable of understanding how wonderful, how unselfish, how dedicated David was, he'd probably only sneer at someone who believed in devoting his life to helping others far less fortunate than himself. And as for that business of the engagement ring—well, naturally David would have bought her one if there'd been time, but it had all happened so fast, just three weeks of quiet dinners, theatre visits, gentle kisses that had sent soft flutters through her heart.

They had packed so much into those three weeks, though; she had sat for hours just listening to him talking about his work as a teacher among the people of the desert, her eyes glowing with admiration as he described a way of life so totally different from anything she'd ever known. It had made her own sheltered existence seem unbearably dull and useless by comparison, and guilt had swept through her when she had compared her own life with David's, realising what a self-centred, indulgent life she'd led until now.

Then one night, after coming out of a restaurant, they had got caught in the rain, and as they had huddled together under David's mac, they'd suddenly found themselves kissing each other.

David had stared at her with near-awe in his eyes after that first gentle touch of their lips.

'You're so beautiful,' he said softly, a little breathlessly. 'Sophie, I just can't imagine life without you. I know I don't have anything to offer you, I'm not rich or successful, but I do love you. Will you marry me?'

Dazed by her admiration for him, still reeling from that strange tingling inside her that his kiss had aroused, at that moment she would have followed him to the ends of the earth, done absolutely anything he'd asked.

'Of course I'll marry you,' she had whispered huskily.

His mouth touched hers again with reverence.

'I'll make you happy, I promise I will,' he told her fervently, and she buried her face against his shoulder and felt humble and grateful that a man like David Stanton should choose her to be his wife.

For the next few days they had wandered around hand in hand, like a couple of children, their good night kisses sweet and gentle. Then, far too soon for both of them, his leave was over and he had had to return to the Sahara and the small school he had founded in the remote desert town of Hajjar. Naturally, he hadn't wanted to go, but he was so conscientious, he wouldn't throw up his job, not even for her. And Sophie had tried to match his unselfish dedication to his work, she'd bitten back all her pleas for him to stay, and had comforted herself with the thought that there was only another year of his contract to run. Then he'd come back to England and they'd be married.

Only she had woken up one morning and thought, why wait? Why not go out and join him right now? Quite apart from the fact that it meant they could be together, David had always been telling her how short-handed he was at the school. Well, she could help him, they'd work together side by side. The thought filled her with a bright glow of satisfaction; for the first time in her life she would be doing something to help others instead of wasting her time on all the frivolous pursuits which had filled her empty days until now.

It hadn't been quite that easy, of course. There'd been visas to obtain, and inoculations, and a few white lies to be told to her parents because, darlings though they were, they had been over-protective of her since the day she was born, and they would have died of shock if they had known their only daughter was running off to the desert to marry a man she had only known for three weeks. Although she'd hated deceiving them, she was sure it was for the best to keep them in the dark for a while. They thought she was staying with her cousin in London for a couple of months while she took a Cordon Bleu cookery course. Her cousin Kate had volunteered to cover for her, and she'd even promised to think of some plausible excuse if her parents kept ringing up and asking to speak to her. In fact, Kate had been thrilled at Sophie's daring venture, and had egged her on when Sophie's courage had flagged slightly at the thought of what she was about to undertake.

And now she was here, and in many ways her journey to this new life had been a lot harder than she'd expected. She was at last beginning to realise how cocooned her life had been up until now. She loved her parents dearly, but she wished now that they had forced her to be more independent, given her a gentle push out of the nest when she had reached her late teens and encouraged her to stand on her own two feet. She had turned up late in their lives, though, when they had just about given up any hope of having a child, and ever since they had cosseted and indulged her, generous with love, with money, with gifts. Their constant support, coupled with her own startlingly good looks, meant that she had had an easy, undemanding ride through life so far.

It wasn't until she'd met David—ironically enough, at a charity affair organised by her mother to raise funds to help educate the under-privileged in third world countries—that she had been forced to take a clear, honest look at herself. And to her shock, she hadn't much liked what she'd seen. Compared to David, who had dedicated his life to helping to eradicate ignorance from the world, she was little more than a butterfly, a beautiful but useless creature, whose only purpose in life was to be an ornament to be gazed at and admired.

From somewhere deep inside her had welled up a burning desire to be *useful*, to make some sort of contribution to the world, even if it was only on a very small scale. Her new-found idealism took root and grew, and somehow it was all mixed up with David himself, his dedication to his work, the bright enthusiasm in his eyes as he described his school, his achievements, the many setbacks he had encountered and his constant struggle to overcome them.

And so here she was, deep in the desert, on her way to join the man who had brought some purpose into her life. Although she had read all the books she could lay her hands on before starting out on this journey, the harshness of this beautiful but vast and desolate land had still come as a shock, and she had been badly upset by the poverty until she had realised that many of these people were nomads, they didn't *need* loads of material possessions. A family that was constantly on the move needed only the basic essentials.

A helpful official had arranged for her to travel to Hajjar with the camel-herders. Then she had fallen sick with that wretched fever, and the camel-herders had panicked and dumped her on Jareth Kingsley, who was clearly less than delighted with her company.

His gaze was resting on her ringless hand again now, as if he still didn't quite believe the story she'd told him. Quite suddenly, she wished that she *did* have a ring there, even if it were only a very cheap one. Anything to wipe that look of scepticism from that dark face.

'This fiancé of yours,' he queried casually, 'are you sure he really loves you?'

'Not that it's any damned business of yours, but yes, he most certainly does,' Sophie snapped back angrily.

'Then what the hell is he doing allowing you to wander around a country like this all by yourself?' he asked quite reasonably.

She scowled.

'He doesn't know I'm coming,' she admitted at last.

The strong mouth curled up fractionally.

'I see. It's to be a surprise. Well, let's just hope that he's the one who's surprised, not you.'

Her eyes flashed.

'And what exactly do you mean by that?' she demanded.

'Men can get very lonely out here,' he observed casually. 'And the Arab girls can be quite startlingly beautiful.'

'Are you suggesting——?' Sophie began to splutter, so furious that she couldn't even finish what she was saying.

Jareth Kingsley merely shrugged.

'These things happen. The desert can be a terribly

lonely place, and I don't suppose this David of yours is a saint.'

'He's the nearest thing to one that I've ever met!' Sophie shot back instantly.

One dark eyebrow rose expressively.

'In that case, I feel rather sorry for you,' he remarked. 'I wouldn't have thought marriage to a saint would be particularly easy—or rewarding.'

She was still trying to think of a crushing reply when he quickly got up and walked away, obviously losing all interest in the conversation. As she watched him go, she was still seething inside and hardly noticed that he was walking with a pronounced limp, as if one leg was very stiff.

His remark about the Arab girls kept echoing round and round inside her head, which had just begun to ache rather badly again. Stubbornly, she pushed it out of her mind. It was ridiculous to think David would ever indulge in such an affair, he just wouldn't, she knew he wouldn't.

She lay back on the blanket and closed her eyes, wishing her headache would go away. Although the fever had broken during the night, she still felt horribly weak, and that encounter with Jareth Kingsley had totally exhausted her. Waves of tiredness rolled over her and with a small sigh she curled up and slid almost immediately into a heavy sleep.

She was finally woken up again by someone roughly shaking her.

'I'm afraid there's no maid to bring your ladyship breakfast in bed,' remarked a familiar sardonic voice. 'And of course, the coffee's a little short on sugar and cream.'

Sophie stared at the tin mug he had set down beside her.

'It can't be any worse than the tea those camel-herders gave me,' she commented glumly, remembering the dark, strong brew and ignoring his deliberately provocative remarks.

After a couple of sips, she brightened up a little.

'Not bad, not bad at all,' she declared. 'What's your cooking like?'

'Very basic. I usually eat when I come to one of the villages.'

'I'm a pretty good cook,' she said hopefully. 'If you took me to Hajjar, I'd promise to do all the meals.'

His face instantly became shuttered.

'We're going to Umra. And after that, we're splitting up, I'm travelling on alone.'

Curiosity stirred inside her.

'Where are you heading for?' she asked.

He hesitated before finally answering.

'Probably north-east, towards Egypt. I'd like to journey up the Nile, visit some of the ancient tombs and temples.'

Sophie looked at him rather indignantly.

'Then you're just what you accused me of being,' she said, a little crossly. 'A tourist who wants to get away from the beaten track.'

'Not exactly,' came his rather curt answer. 'A tourist usually knows precisely where he's going. I'm just—wandering.'

Something in his tone alerted her, set her quick mind to work.

'Wandering—or running away?' she wondered out loud.

His face instantly became blank, nothing showed in his eyes except one brief angry spark which he quickly, deliberately extinguished.

'We'll be leaving in ten minutes,' he informed her

coldly. 'You'd better get yourself ready.'

He strode away, and this time his limp registered more strongly on Sophie's inquisitive mind. As she disentangled herself from the blanket, then stood up on legs that were still precariously wobbly after the fever, a hundred and one questions began to run through her active brain. Then she gave a resigned sigh. It was beginning to look as if she wasn't going to get a chance to find out any of the answers. The future had been mapped out for her pretty clearly. Jareth Kingsley was going to dump her at Umra, like a piece of unwanted luggage, and then go on without her.

Her own bundle of posessions had already been loaded on to the camel, which was sitting nearby, glaring at her every bit as fiercely as Jareth Kingsley did when she said something that annoyed him. Sophie had mixed feelings about camels. They spat, they smelt, they often had vile tempers, yet there was something unashamedly romantic about riding through the desert on the back of one of these great lumbering beasts. And there was no denying that they were the most practical form of transport in this hot, harsh land.

'Are you ready?' enquired Jareth Kingsley with a touch of impatience.

She gave a small nod, then clambered inexpertly on to the back of the sitting camel, clutching at the saddlehorn as she wriggled into place. Then an involuntary shiver ran through her as Jareth swung himself lithely into place behind her. The saddle was meant to take one, not two, so his body fitted very snugly against hers, hips and chest pressing hard against her back, thigh and calf matching the line of her own so exactly that they almost seemed to merge into one, making her blink slightly dizzily, leaving her with

the weird impression that she couldn't quite tell where
her own body ended and his began.

It's the fever, she told herself shakily. She was
obviously still weak and lightheaded, perhaps even
hallucinating slightly. It was the only explanation for
this really odd *melting* sensation that had crept over her
ever since Jareth Kingsley had swung himself into the
saddle.

Then the camel heaved itself awkwardly to its feet,
and the violent jolting sent all other thoughts flying
straight out of her head as she concentrated on hanging
on to the saddlehorn. Glad that she hadn't disgraced
herself by falling off, she settled down again as the
camel plodded off and rather grimly tried to ignore the
pressing physical presence of the man behind her.

She almost succeeded—but not quite. And she found
herself suddenly eager to reach Umra. It didn't matter
that this man wouldn't take her to Hajjar, she'd find
some way to get there, and she was longing—*longing*—
to see David, of course she was. She could see his face
now, the fair hair, the pale blue eyes. At least, she could
almost see it, somehow it was peculiarly blurred around
the edges, like an out-of-focus photograph, and that
worried her until she convinced herself that it was just
another after-effect of that wretched fever.

The camel plodded on over the amber sand, and the
heat shimmered all around them in undulating waves
that reduced everything around them to a softly pulsing
golden haze. Nothing seemed quite real, not the endless
stretches of sand, the dark outlines of the thorn-bushes,
the towers of rock that had been sculpted by the fierce
wind that could scour the desert, or the mountains that
danced elusively in the distance, their shape and colour
distorted by the hot air that rose in giant ripples from
the desert floor. The sun got hotter and hotter, beating

down on them from a turquoise sky, and Sophie gradually grew more and more dozy, heavy-limbed. After a while her eyes closed, she relaxed back, lulled by the rhythmic gait of the slow-moving animal.

Then, without even knowing it had happened, she slid into a deep sleep, held safe in the arms of Jareth Kingsley.

CHAPTER TWO

She woke up with a start, and felt hot, achy, uncomfortably stiff. It was a couple of minutes before she could even remember where she was, then it all came slowly tumbling back into her mind and her muscles tensed as she became starkly aware of the hard male body behind her.

'Why have we stopped?' she asked a little woozily, realising that it was the lack of movement from the camel that had finally awoken her. She glanced around. They were in a *wadi*, a dried-up river bed. After the rains, water would flow where they were now standing, but there was only sand and hard, cracked mud under the camel's feet now. More important, though, there were acacia trees and thorn-bushes which would provide welcome patches of shade.

'It's late afternoon,' Jareth told her. 'There's no point in travelling further today. We're still quite a long way from Umra, we can't possibly reach it before nightfall.'

Sophie yawned.

'How long have I been asleep?'

'Several hours. How do you feel?'

His unexpectedly considerate question surprised her and made her wonder if he might not be halfway human after all.

'Much better,' she said, quite truthfully. Her long sleep really seemed to have done her good. 'But I'm awfully thirsty,' she added.

He helped her dismount, then began to unload the camel. After a couple of minutes, he turned to face her.

'This would take far less time if you lent a hand,' he remarked rather pointedly. 'Or are you so used to being waited on hand and foot that you expect me to act as your servant?'

She flushed heavily.

'Why do you have to keep being so thoroughly unpleasant?'

The dark brows drew together in that familiar expression of irritability.

'Perhaps because I hadn't counted on being saddled with a spoilt little brat who likes getting her own way far too much,' he growled.

Sophie stamped her foot.

'Why do you keep saying all these horrible things about me? You don't even know me! You can't possibly know what I'm really like!'

Too late, she realised that her explosive outburst had probably only served to reinforce his low opinion of her. But the man really was quite impossible, it would take a saint not to respond to his provocative remarks. And although she'd led a far more sheltered life than most people would ever have guessed, she most definitely wasn't a candidate for sainthood.

Then she stopped worrying altogether about his opinion of her, because he was looming over her now, those vivid blue eyes blazing with undisguised exasperation.

'So I don't know what you're really like?' he challenged. 'Well, first impressions are usually pretty reliable. And just about the first thing you did when you came out of that fever was to demand that I take you to Hajjar. Not a word about whether I had any plans of my own, if it might be inconvenient for me to go miles and miles out of my way. Oh no, my lady, all you were concerned about were your own problems and how you could use me to solve them.'

'It wasn't like that,' she protested weakly. 'It wasn't!'

'No? Well, it damned well seemed like it to me.'

And with that, he set about unloading the rest of his baggage from the camel, leaving her to stare miserably at his strong back as she tried to convince herself that there hadn't been a single word of truth in his accusations.

Finally admitting that she might have been just a fraction in the wrong, she shuffled reluctantly over to join him.

'What can I do to help?' she asked in a small voice.

He rummaged around in a saddlebag, finally producing a tin of stew and some rather stale bread.

'You said you could cook,' he reminded her. 'I've no idea if you were lying or not, but not even you could make a mess of heating up tinned stew. Here, catch!'

He tossed the tin over to her and she caught it, staring at it doubtfully.

'You'll find a saucepan, tin-opener, everything else you need, over there,' he told her, pointing to another pile of equipment.

She had seen the camel-herders lighting a fire several times and it hadn't looked too difficult. While Jareth finished unloading the camel and then hobbled its front legs with a leather thong so that it could move about grazing, but wouldn't be able to wander too far, she set about collecting pieces of bone-dry wood. Poking around in the saddlebag, she found a small metal tripod on which to balance the saucepan, and with the help of a box of matches and a handful of dry straw, she finally got the fire going. With the saucepan of stew perched over the flames, she sat back on her heels, a faint flush of success colouring her skin.

'Not bad,' remarked Jareth with a touch of surprise

as he squatted down beside her.

'You mean not bad for a useless society brat,' Sophie tossed back at him accusingly.

To her utter astonishment, he actually smiled. The result was absolutely amazing. The dark blue eyes briefly danced into life, the hard mouth relaxed into a warmly sensual line and that frighteningly remote expression simply faded away.

'You should smile more often,' she said, without thinking. 'It makes you look completely different.'

The smile instantly vanished, he turned his head away so she couldn't see his face.

'Life doesn't seem particularly amusing at the moment,' he responded with the abruptness to which she was fast becoming accustomed. He reached for one of the waterskins. 'Are you still thirsty?' he asked, deliberately changing the subject.

Quickly smothering the impulse to ask a whole lot of questions which she knew he wouldn't answer and which would only annoy him, she nodded, then wrinkled her nose.

'I just wish the water didn't taste so foul. It always seems to have that dreadful tarry taste.'

'I know a remedy for that.'

Sophie watched in fascination as he measured a small amount of flour and sugar into the water. After whisking it round, he then poured it into her mug.

'Try that,' he invited.

Rather dubiously, she took a small sip, then one eyebrow shot up in surprise.

'It's not bad. Really quite refreshing.'

'It's a trick I learnt from the Arabs,' he told her. 'They call it *habsha*.'

They drank and ate in unexpectedly companionable silence, softening the stale bread by using it to mop up the last of the gravy from the stew. It was probably the simplest meal Sophie had ever eaten, yet in an odd way it was also one of the most satisfying. The desert had a way of reducing everything to basics, she reflected as she scoured the plates with sand to clean them. There simply wasn't room for any frills or luxuries, survival was everything in this harsh world. Enough water, enough food were the priorities, with water being the absolutely basic essential. With a camel for transport, a thick blanket to keep you warm during the unexpectedly cold nights, you had virtually everything you needed.

When he had finished eating, Jareth took a battered paperback from his saddlebag—a popular thriller, Sophie noticed—and began to read. She had brought a couple of books herself, but this evening she wasn't in the mood for reading. Instead she sat back and let her gaze drift over the desolate scene in front of her, the amber sand, the golden yellow of the coarse grass, in the distance the broken craggy outline of hills. The sun swelled to a huge orange globe as evening drew in, touching everything with its dying radiance, and she caught her breath lightly at the terrifyingly beautiful desolation.

Then the sun began to sink with its usual swiftness, and all its warmth swiftly vanished with the dying light. She pulled on a thick sweater, reached for a blanket. It was too dark for Jareth to read any longer, so he tossed his book aside and fetched his own blanket.

'Better sleep now, we'll be making an early start in the morning,' he advised. 'If everything goes well, we should reach Umra late in the afternoon.'

'You just can't wait to get rid of me, can you?' she snapped, her earlier good mood swiftly vanishing.

'I didn't ask for your company in the first place,' came his cool reminder.

'I know, I'm just a nuisance. You've made that perfectly clear,' she muttered resentfully, burrowing further under the blanket, then dragging it tightly around her. 'I suppose you're the original lone wolf, you don't need anyone.'

It was several seconds before he answered her.

'Everyone needs someone,' he said at last. 'But there are also times when you need to be on your own.'

Sophie wasn't in a mood to be easily placated.

'A lone wolf,' she muttered again. 'Just my luck, to run across the one person in the whole of the Sahara who wants to live like a hermit!'

And with that she pulled the blanket over her head, closed her eyes tight, and resolutely tried to go to sleep.

Despite the hardness of the ground and the chill of the night, which penetrated even the thickness of the blanket, she finally dropped off. For a while she had a couple of mixed-up, weird dreams, full of camels and wolves and mysterious figures drifting along in the distance, then she slipped into a period of deeper, more restful sleep. Then someone started shouting, and for a few confused seconds she thought she had started dreaming again, only her eyes were wide open, she was staring up at the velvet sky with its pattern of incredibly bright stars, the softly glowing orb of the moon.

The shouting had died down, become muted to a tormented cry.

'Oh no—Oh God, *no*!'

The tortured tone of voice chilled her blood, sent goosebumps racing over her prickling skin. Dragging her blanket off, Sophie scrambled over to Jareth, who was lying a few yards away.

The pale light of the moon shone directly down on to his sweat-slicked face, his hair clinging damply to his skin as his head tossed from side to side.

'Why me?' he murmured hoarsely. 'Why me, not them? All my fault, all my fault——'

Realising he was deep in the grip of some horrific nightmare, she grabbed his shoulder, tried frantically to shake him out of it. He couldn't seem to break free of it, though, he physically fought her as she tried to force him awake, grabbing hold of her wrists, digging his fingers deep into her skin until she cried out with pain. Half falling across him, feeling the heat of his twisting body right through the blanket that still covered him, Sophie yelled his name, slightly desperately tried to break free of his punishing grip.

His eyes suddenly shot open, he stared blankly up at her as if she were a ghost, part of the nightmare that racked him.

Sophie dragged in a shuddering breath, then another.

'Jareth, it's me—Sophie,' she somehow managed to get out at last. 'Please—let go of my wrists. You're hurting me.'

His gaze swivelled downwards, he stared with fascinated horror at his own long, strong fingers pressing cruelly into her delicate skin. With a tiny gasp, he released her, and raised his hands to cover his eyes.

Sophie rubbed her aching wrists ruefully.

'Wow, when you have bad dreams, you really do go all the way, don't you?' she said in a much steadier voice. 'What on earth was it all about?'

'I don't remember,' he muttered, his eyes still hidden behind his locked fingers.

Both of them knew perfectly well that he was lying, but Sophie had sense enough not to push it any further. Sitting back on her heels, she looked down at him.

'Your shirt's soaked with sweat,' she said more practically. 'I'll find you a dry one.'

'I don't need mothering!' Jareth growled irritably.

She regarded him steadily.

'Perhaps what you need is a good psychiatrist,' she suggested in a low voice.

His hands shot away from his face, the full force of those baleful blue eyes rested directly on her.

'Perhaps what I need is to be left in peace, not have some damned stranger poking her nose into something that's absolutely none of her business!'

It was starting to hurt somewhere deep inside her when he tore into her like that. And that was a little scarey because no one had ever had that effect on her before.

Something must have showed on her face, because he suddenly raked his fingers through his sweat-soaked hair and released an unexpectedly rueful sigh.

'Okay, I'm sorry,' he apologised in a much softer tone. 'Just because I get bad dreams, there's no need to take it out on you.'

That last remark registered instantly on her quick mind.

'You get bad dreams often? The same dream?' she queried with a concerned frown.

For a moment, she thought he was going to say something. He looked almost as if he desperately needed to talk to someone. Then that shuttered look came over his face again and he half turned away.

'Look, I've already said I'm sorry for waking you up, and grabbing hold of you. Let's just leave it at that, shall we?' He paused briefly, then lifted his head, his dark brows drawing together in sudden concern. 'Did I hurt your arms?'

'Not very much.'

'Let me see them.'

Reluctantly, Sophie held them out, heard the breath hiss lightly in his throat as he saw the dark fingermarks

on her skin. Not even the subdued moonlight masked
the vividness of the imprints.

'They'll soon fade,' she assured him valiantly.

'Do they hurt?'

'Not much.'

'Liar,' he accused softly, as he sat up and examined
them carefully. 'Here, perhaps I can do something to
help. Just sit still and let your arms relax.'

He held her wrists in the warm palms of his hands.
Then, using just his thumb and fingertips, he began to
lightly massage the bruised skin. It was a gentle,
soothing, rather delicious sensation, that light, constant
friction of his skin against her own, and Sophie
involuntarily closed her eyes, feeling tiny threads of
pleasure begin to creep right up her arms, into her body,
filling her with a strange tingly sensation. They were
touching nowhere else, only at the wrists, but even that
brief point of contact was suddenly quite overwhelming. Unnerved, she wrenched her arms out of his grasp.

'That's—that's much better. You can stop now,' she
gasped. With some trepidation, she risked a glance at
him from under her thick lashes. Then she blinked with
amazement as she realised he hadn't even noticed her
disturbed reaction. And he certainly hadn't experienced
anything even remotely like it himself.

Careful, Sophie, she warned herself shakily. Don't let
your imagination run away with you. Okay, so you felt
really funny for a moment, but it's probably just shock,
being woken up so suddenly and then being practically
assaulted. Something like that's bound to have a bit of
an effect on you. It doesn't *mean* anything, though, so
just forget about it, put it right out of your head.

A little too hurriedly, she scrambled to her feet.

'I'll fetch your dry shirt,' she told him. She had the
feeling it would be much easier to put all this in

perspective if she could just get away from him for a couple of minutes. Taking much longer than was necessary to find his spare shirt, she finally dawdled back to him, only to find that he'd already stripped off the damp shirt and was towelling the last of the sweat from his body.

Under the shirt he was wearing the cotton trousers which most Arabs wore, loose-fitting around the thighs but tight around the ankles, which made them ideal for riding. Above the white cotton, the dark skin of his chest and arms glistened in the moonlight, the texture of fine silk. Only a cluster of dark hair marred its smoothness, spreading from nipple to nipple and then arrowing down his stomach, disappearing tantalisingly beneath the waist of the trousers.

As she stared at him, Sophie felt herself grow hot, peculiarly disorientated. There was a funny unsteadiness in her legs and her palms felt uncomfortably clammy. And those bruises on her wrists throbbed with a steady rhythm, not painfully but with a light, insistent pulsing, a constant reminder of the man who had put them there.

More after-effects of her fever? she asked herself in growing alarm. Yes, it *had* to be. There couldn't possibly be any other explanation.

Jareth pulled on the dry shirt, then glanced at her briefly.

'Better get back to bed,' he told her. 'There's still time for a few more hours' sleep before morning.'

She tried to swallow and found her throat was very dry.

'Will you—will you be all right now?' she croaked.

'Fine,' he answered firmly, although she was left with the impression that he was finding it much harder than he had expected to keep his voice completely steady.

Somehow, she managed to drag her gaze away from him and stumbled back to where she had left her own blanket. Lying down and wrapping its thickness around her still shaky limbs, she shot a furtive glance in Jareth's direction and found that he was now lying down again, but with his hands behind his head and his eyes wide open. To her relief, he wasn't looking at her. He was staring up at the stars, but she guessed that he wasn't seeing them either, but was instead gazing at a series of pictures inside his head. She also guessed that he wouldn't risk sleeping again tonight, not after that horrific nightmare.

And she didn't sleep, either. She lay absolutely still, though, so that he wouldn't know she was still awake, sharing his lonely vigil as, together yet apart, they waited for the first warming glow of the morning sun.

They were on the move almost before the early morning chill had left the air. Neither of them had spoken about last night and Sophie had put on a jumper which had covered the darkening bruises that patterned her lower arms and wrists. Underneath, she wore a thin cotton blouse, because the jumper would become far too hot once the full heat of the day began to beat down on them. A pair of cotton jeans and sturdy sandals completed her outfit. What she missed more than anything was feeling clean. Water was so precious out here that there was rarely more than the smallest amount to spare for washing. And her hair, her crowning glory, which David loved so much and would run his fingers through again and again in silent admiration, felt lank and dust-filled, the glorious apricot colour dulled, its full beauty hidden because she'd twisted the long strands into a childish but practical plait. David—just saying his name to herself made her feel warm inside. She would be reunited with him soon, very soon, and she smiled contentedly to herself at the prospect.

The camel plodded on, padding along surefootedly, encouraged by an occasional soft clicking sound from Jareth. A couple of hours drifted past, then Sophie's sharp eyes spotted a cloud of dust in the distance.

'What's that?' she asked with interest.

'I'm not sure,' frowned Jareth. 'But it seems to be coming our way, so we'll soon find out.'

The dust cloud drifted nearer, then thinned a little in the light breeze, so that they could make out the blurred shape of a string of camels. The camels were heavily laden with household items; food and cooking gear, tent-poles and rolls of canvas, and water in great pots mounted on wooden frames. Riding alongside them were men mounted not on camels, but on small stallions. Some of the men were carrying javelins, the tips glittering brightly in the dazzling sunshine. And behind the camels came a flock of goats, bleating noisily as they trotted through the smoke-screen of dust which had been thrown up by the camels and stallions in front of them.

Sophie gazed in fascination at the colourful spectacle. 'Who are they?' she asked, twisting round to look at Jareth.

'One of the nomadic tribes moving south to their winter grazing grounds,' he answered her, as fascinated as she was by the pageant winding its way towards them. 'Look,' he went on as the procession drew even nearer, 'see how the women and children are travelling?'

Sophie's gaze skipped along to the small caravan that led the long, straggling procession. These camels carried litters on their backs, ornate structures which were draped with brilliant silk veils and hand-made carpets patterned with intricate designs. Now and then she would catch a brief glimpse of a pale face inside the litters, or would see an inquisitive child poking its head out through the silk draperies to take a peep at the world outside. And the camels themselves were decked out as splendidly as the litters they carried. Head dresses of jet-black ostrich plumes tossed in the breeze, plaited and tasselled leather necklaces swung from their heads and necks, and streamers tumbled from their saddlebags.

'It's fantastic!' she exclaimed excitedly.

'Yes, it is,' agreed Jareth, but there was a slightly thoughtful note in his voice now, as if his mind had just slid off along another track. A moment later, he urged his own camel forward, heading towards the procession of nomads.

A couple of men on stallions rode over to greet him, and although Sophie had studiously learnt some basic Arabic before setting out on this journey and had picked up quite a lot of useful phrases since arriving here, she couldn't follow the quick exchange between Jareth and the nomads.

At one point there seemed to be a fairly long session of bargaining going on, and she frowned, wondering what on earth Jareth was up to this time.

She didn't have to wait long to find out.

As the bartering came to a close, the two nomads beamed and nodded in agreement. Behind her, Jareth gave a small grunt of satisfaction, then he slid down from the camel and began to unfasten her bundle of possessions, which was tied to the saddle.

'What's happening?' she demanded with just a trace of alarm.

'You've still got plenty of money, haven't you?' asked

Jareth as he finished unloading her things from the camel.

'You know I have,' she flung back at him accusingly. 'You went through all my things, you probably counted every penny of it while you were at it!'

'Well, I've just spent some of it for you,' he told her calmly. 'For a very reasonable sum, these nomads are going to take you south with them.'

His cool assumption that he had the right to tell her what to do, where to go, completely infuriated her.

'But I don't want to go south! I'm going to join David at Hajjar, and Hajjar's to the north, you *know* that!'

Jareth raised his head to confront her, the vivid blue eyes blazing with irritation.

'Cut it out, Sophie,' he ordered. 'You've had your adventure and by some miracle you've managed to get this far without getting hurt, but no one's luck holds out for ever. The Sahara's no place for a girl on her own, especially someone like you, who's had it soft all her life. This is a harsh, often cruel place, God knows how you've managed to survive here this long. Now's the time to call it quits, though. In four or five days this tribe will be passing close to a fairly large town where you'll be able to get some motor transport. Hire someone to drive you back to civilisation, then catch the first plane back to England, where you belong.'

She wriggled off the camel's back and slithered to the ground, then she flicked back her heavy plait and glared at him.

'Will you stop trying to organise my life for me?' she gritted. 'I know exactly what I'm doing, I don't need you to make my decisions for me!'

He kept a tight rein on his own temper, which somehow only made her even more angry.

'It's pretty obvious that you *don't* know what you're

doing, or else you wouldn't be here,' he told her forcefully. 'Heaven knows what your parents were thinking of, allowing you to go off on this wild-goose chase. Well, maybe they don't give a damn about you, but I do, while you're travelling with me you're my responsibility.'

She stamped her foot furiously.

'I am not your responsibility!' she hissed. 'And how dare you insinuate that my parents don't care about me! They love me very much, they've always given me everything I've ever wanted.'

One dark eyebrow lifted expressively.

'That probably explains why you've turned out so stubborn and spoilt,' he commented. 'But we're not here to argue about your family life, I'm only interested in getting you back to safety. And don't stamp your foot at me again,' he warned slightly grimly. 'I'm in no mood to deal with your tantrums right now. Grow up, Sophie, stop behaving like a five-year-old who's throwing a fit of temper because she can't get her own way over something.'

A brief wave of shame swept over her. She knew she was behaving badly, but she just couldn't seem to help it. There was something about this man that brought out the worst in her, she decided ruefully. He sparked off something deep inside her, a volatile reaction that she just didn't know how to control.

She took a deep breath, tried hard to calm herself.

'Look, let's talk this over——' she began in a much more reasonable tone.

'There's nothing to discuss,' he cut in. 'You're not being given any choice, it's already been arranged. You'll travel in one of the litters, and the women of the tribe will look after you. You'll be perfectly safe. Of course, I can't force you to go back to England, but I'd

strongly advise it. Forget about going to Hajjar, Sophie,'
he warned. 'If your fiancé loves you as much as you say
he does, he won't want you to kill yourself trying to
reach him.'

'What if I refuse to go? If I just stay here?' she
demanded, planting both feet on the ground and staring
at him rebelliously.

'Then you'll be behaving more stupidly than even I
thought you were capable of,' he answered evenly. 'I
don't think you'll do that, though. You're not lacking in
intelligence, even though your manners do leave a lot to
be desired at times.'

He remounted his camel, let his dark blue gaze rest
steadily on her for several seconds.

'You've had your adventure and it must have taken a
lot of guts for you to get this far by yourself,' he went on
with unexpected gentleness. 'But this is the end of the
road, Sophie. Go home and wait for your fiancé there.
And tell him he's a lucky man to have found a girl who
loves him enough to follow him halfway round the
world to a wilderness like this.'

Leaving her gaping slightly with surprise, he clicked
softly to the camel, which obediently lumbered off. For
a while, she stood and watched him go, her gaze fixed
on his straight-backed figure, a small part of her hoping
vainly that he would glance back just once. He kept
staring fixedly ahead, though, and a minute later she
jumped slightly as one of the nomads touched her lightly
on the arm.

She didn't understand what he was saying, but he was
gesturing towards one of the litters and it was clear this
was the one she was to travel in. As the camel bearing
the litter knelt, she climbed up inside, smiling shyly at
the young, dark-haired woman who was already sitting
there. The woman murmured a greeting under her

breath, then the camel was clambering to its feet again and they were moving off southwards, away from Hajjar and David—away from Jareth Kingsley.

The woman whose litter she was sharing made no attempt at any conversation. Instead, she sat with her head slightly averted, as if a little in awe of this stranger who had been almost literally dumped in her lap. For her own part, Sophie felt completely depressed. She'd failed, she wasn't going to see David after all, watch his eyes light up with pleasure when he found her standing on his doorstep. She tried hard to picture his eyes, that pale blue, smiling gaze, and instead found her memory would only conjure up a vivid image of bright blue eyes that stared at her remotely, tantalising her with their blankness, their haunting emptiness.

'Oh, go away,' she muttered crossly under her breath.

The Arab woman glanced at her curiously and Sophie grinned sheepishly.

'Just talking to myself,' she said, but the woman merely looked uneasy, as if she were a little worried at having to share her litter with this English girl who was obviously a trifle touched in the head.

Despite the sumptuous trappings, it was stuffy inside the litter, and not particularly comfortable. The thought of having to spend another four of five days, perhaps even longer, in its claustrophobic confines filled Sophie with gloom. A little desperately, she set her mind to work on the problem, considering several wild alternatives. Then one of them didn't seem quite as wild as all the others—a bit risky, perhaps, but anything would be better than sitting in this litter for days on end, then meekly trotting off home to England, abandoning all the bright hopes and dreams that had brought her out here in the first place.

Sticking her head out through the silk curtains that

veiled the litter, she saw one of the men riding near by and she vigorously waved her arms at him. He merely looked puzzled, so she gestured to him to come nearer and at last he seemed to cotton on, and manouevred his horse over to the camel's side.

Searching through her strictly limited Arabic vocabulary, Sophie at last managed to come up with what she hoped was the right phrase.

'I want to buy a camel,' she said very clearly.

The nomad looked so amazed that for a moment she wondered if she'd said the wrong word, anxiously checked over the Arabic phrase again in her mind to make sure she'd got it right.

'A camel,' she repeated. 'I want to buy a camel.'

The nomad turned his head, glanced at the herd of camels that, along with the goats, brought up the rear of the caravan, and she released a sigh of relief, certain that he had understood her.

He muttered something under his breath, looked doubtful, and for a moment she thought he was going to refuse her request outright. Then he called out to a couple of the other men, and the entire procession gradually wound to a halt, several more nomads galloping up to see what was happening while the women peered curiously out from their litters, staring with interest at this girl who was causing this unscheduled interruption to their journey.

It was pretty obvious that they were reluctant to sell her a camel, although she didn't know if it was because they disapproved of a woman riding off into the desert on her own or if they simply didn't want to part with one of their animals. And since she couldn't understand more than a word or two of what they were saying, it was hard to work out exactly what was going on inside their heads.

In the end, though, they seemed to decide to let the mad English girl have her own way. That settled, everyone gathered round to listen to the haggling over the price, which was to include a saddle, a couple of waterskins and a small supply of food. Since Sophie had had to haggle over every single item she had bought since her arrival, she entered into the whole thing enthusiastically, finally beating them down to a price she hoped was reasonable. From the slightly smug looks on the faces of the nomads, she guessed she was still paying well above the market price of the camel, but she couldn't afford to hang around any longer. With every minute that passed, Jareth was getting further and further away from her. She had to leave at once if she was to have any hope of catching him up.

At last she was settled on her camel, which fortunately seemed to be fairly docile. She waved goodbye to the nomads, then she headed the camel northwards and began to trek along the trail which Jareth had taken a few hours earlier.

Her plan was quite simple: to stick to the trail until she finally caught up with him. She was sure he wouldn't have travelled too far, he hadn't been in a particular hurry. She reckoned if she pressed on hard she'd catch up with him some time later this evening.

At the thought of seeing him again, a small quiver of excitement wriggled its way along her nerve-ends, a faint glow of colour touched her face. Of course, he wouldn't be particularly pleased to see her, at least not at first, but his bad temper probably wouldn't last for long. And with luck, she'd be able to talk him round, eventually persuade him to take her to Hajjar. Men nearly always did what she wanted, it was something to do with her looks, she supposed. Full of confidence, she urged the camel to a faster pace, keeping her eyes glued to the roughly marked trail so that she wouldn't get lost.

She turned round once, just in time to see the caravan of nomads disappearing into the distance. Then the next time she glanced back, they had gone, with only a faint cloud of dust hanging in the still air to mark their passing.

For the first time, she was totally alone in the desert. Slightly uneasily, she tried to make the camel go even faster. She wasn't scared, of course she wasn't, but the sooner she caught up with Jareth, the better.

The trail was hard to follow, nearly disappearing in places under drifts of red sand. And on either side of the trail, the desert stretched out in a kaleidoscope of colour, orange and scarlet and brown, with hummocks of red-ochre rock, the dark gold of the stunted tufts of dried grass and, in the distance, a shimmering wedge of grey mountains. But it was the emptiness that finally got to her, the sheer immensity of it that overwhelmed her, making her feel so small, so totally insignificant. She would have given anything for the sight of another human being, but nothing stirred in that vast stretch of desolation except a giant vulture which perched in a thorn-tree and watched her pass with a chilling glare. Despite the heat, shivers ran right through Sophie's body. That vulture was a stark reminder of what happened to careless travellers who strayed from the trail and fell victim to this cruelly beautiful land.

After a couple of hours, the sun began to slither towards the horizon and the desert became drenched with gold, while the sky blazed with crimson, pink and burnt sienna, splashed across a background of dark turquoise. Knowing how quickly it would get dark, Sophie gritted her teeth to stop them chattering. She had to be close to Jareth now, she just *had* to be.

'Come on, Sophie, don't give up yet,' she muttered to

herself fiercely. 'He can't be far ahead. Just keep going——'

Her voice trailed away as she heard the sound of muffled hoofbeats behind her. She twisted round in the saddle and her eyes flew wide open with alarm as she saw two men galloping towards her, reining their horses in hard as they reached her, kicking up small spurts of dust. Their dark gaze swept over her with fast-growing interest, then they exchanged brief comments in Arabic, speaking too swiftly for her to follow. As she noticed the rifles they carried, her heart began to thud out a frantic rhythm and sweat trickled down her rigid spine.

Bandits? They certainly looked fierce enough. And they hadn't offered the polite, ritual greeting which all desert travellers exchanged upon meeting.

'W-what do you want?' she quavered, trying valiantly to hide her fright, but feeling fear begin to ooze out of every pore.

They didn't even answer. Instead, they manoeuvred their horses into position, one on each side of her, then took hold of the reins of her camel.

'What are you doing?' she whispered in dread. Tales she'd heard about the bandits that roamed this region flickered through her head; she wished she'd listened to Jareth's advice, to everyone who had warned her of the dangers of travelling alone in this harsh, lawless land. Instead, she had pigheadedly ploughed on, as determined as always to have her own way. Oh, Sophie, you've been stupid, so *stupid*! she told herself in silent recognition of her own blind foolishness.

Then the two men were leading her away from the trail, ignoring her frantic protests, dragging her off to an unknown destination.

CHAPTER THREE

THEY travelled on for maybe fifteen, twenty minutes, although to Sophie, caught in the grip of sheer terror, it seemed more like hours. Then, through fear-blurred eyes, she saw a *wadi* ahead of them, with several large tents scattered around and a string of horses tethered nearby. Camp-fires had been lit, the flames bright in the swiftly-gathering dusk, and she trembled as the two men brought her camel to a halt, made it sit and then gestured to her to dismount.

Legs shaking helplessly, she did as they ordered, stumbling after them as they made their way towards the largest of the tents.

The flaps were drawn aside, but she scarcely noticed the sumptuousness of the interior, the thick carpet which covered the floor, a protection against the hardness and chill of the ground underneath, or the exquisitely patterned cloth which hung from the walls. Instead, her gaze was riveted on the man seated on a low bed piled with cushions at the far end of the tent.

To her utter astonishment, when he finally spoke, it was in excellent English.

'And what prize have you brought me this time, Ahmed?' he murmured.

The man beside her spoke at some length in Arabic. The black-eyed man on the couch listened, but his gaze never left Sophie's face.

'Who are you?' she managed to get out shakily at last, as the flow of Arabic at last came to an end. 'And why

47

have you brought me here? Have I—have I been kidnapped?'

The black eyes narrowed, the thin, cruel mouth curled into a shadow of a smile.

'Kidnapped, my dear young lady? Most certainly not. I am Sheik Rashid Oman Hissein and you are my honoured guest.'

Despite his cultured tone, there was a distinct air of menace in the tent and his gaze had slid from her face and was now fixed on her hair.

'You must excuse me staring,' he apologised smoothly, 'but I have never seen such hair—the colour is quite magnificent. I would give much to see it hanging loose, in all its glory.'

Something in his voice alerted her to the danger she was now in, and her skin prickled with fresh terror. That last remark, casual as it had sounded on the surface, had been too much like a discreetly worded invitation. And if the invitation failed, she thought slightly desperately, how long would it be before it became a command?

'You speak excellent English,' she babbled, trying frantically to distract him.

He nodded, obviously pleased by her remark.

'I was educated in your country,' he told her. 'It is a not uncommon custom amongst some of our wealthier families. But I digress. We were talking about *you*, my dear young lady. Such beauty,' he said softly, 'you must forgive me if I am overwhelmed, but our own women are all so dark. It is rare in this country to come face to face with someone like yourself, whose hair shines like the sun in the first glow of morning.'

His oily compliments made her shudder, she just wanted to get out of here.

'Well, it was nice to meet you, but I really can't stay,'

she blurted out hurriedly. 'I've arranged to meet someone, I'll be late if I don't leave straightaway.'

An ingratiating smile spread across his face.

'Leave, my dear young lady? But I couldn't possibly allow that. It's nearly dark, and there are so many dangers for someone travelling alone at night.'

Sophie grimly fought back the urge to cry with fright. Tears weren't going to help in the least, she had to use her brains to get herself out of this. Only it wasn't going to be easy, in fact she had a terrible feeling that she was in desperate trouble.

'I told you, I'm meeting someone,' she insisted with renewed determination. 'They're waiting for me, a little further along the trail.'

'You could so easily miss them in the dark,' answered the Sheik silkily. 'No, you must stay here tonight, then continue your journey in the morning. We shall have our evening meal together—and perhaps you would honour me by wearing that beautiful hair of yours loose, so that I can admire its magnificence.'

Caught fast in the throes of deep apprehension, Sophie didn't hear the slight disturbance behind her, the faint current of cool night air as the tent flaps swished open, then closed again. Then a firm hand clasped her shoulder from behind and she smelt the fresh, musky tang of a male body standing only inches away from her.

'This lady wears her hair loose for no one except me,' stated Jareth in a calm yet totally authoritative voice. 'She happens to be my wife.'

There was no mistaking the look of angry frustration that flickered briefly across the Sheik's flushed face. Then it swiftly vanished, he was smoothly urbane again.

'If this lady is indeed your wife, I find it a little strange that you should allow her to travel alone in this

dangerous country,' he commented, staring hard at
Jareth, suspicion shining clearly in his eyes.

'There was an unfortunate mix-up, we became
separated by mistake,' answered Jareth, his voice still
cool, totally controlled. 'My fault, sweetheart,' he went
on in a suddenly more apologetic tone, sliding one
finger under Sophie's chin, gently forcing it up so she
had no choice except to look directly at him. The blue
gaze was so close that she melted under its brilliance.
Her legs, already sagging with relief at her miraculous
rescue, started to shake in earnest as his head bent still
further, warm lips ravaged hers in a kiss that was
deliberately sensual, brief yet scalding, the kind of kiss
that only a lover would give.

Instinctively, she responded, and a sweet abandonment crept through her limbs, she swayed against him,
felt his hand slide round her waist to steady her, his
fingers lying warm against her body, their grip strong
and sure.

Then it was over, leaving her flushed, overheated,
still leaning weakly against Jareth for support.

Slowly, painfully, reality filtered back into her
fevered brain. Don't be a fool, Sophie, she warned
herself shakily. This is all a charade, a silly pantomime
to convince this lecherous sheik that I'm Jareth's wife
and so not available. Just play your part for as long as
you have to, but don't get carried away. It was just a
kiss, that was all, not some earth-shattering revelation.

Which was all very well in theory, but her body was
still vibrating like a leaf in a storm, her legs felt so weak
she could hardly stand up. She might have collapsed
completely if Jareth's hand hadn't continued to support
her steadily.

'Now that I've found my wife, we'll take our leave of
you,' he said casually. 'I am very grateful to you for

taking such good care of her.'

The Sheik's black eyes flashed briefly.

'I cannot let you leave, it would be dangerous for you to travel further tonight. I insist that you accept my hospitality, then you can continue your journey tomorrow, when you are fully rested.'

To Sophie's surprise, Jareth didn't argue. Instead, he merely inclined his head.

'We would be honoured to accept your hospitality,' he answered courteously.

'Good,' replied the Sheik with obvious satisfaction. 'I shall arrange for a tent to be made ready for you. In the meantime, perhaps you would join me in a meal.'

Sophie was beginning to feel as if she were dreaming. That kiss must have made her lightheaded, she told herself woozily as she found herself sitting on soft cushions, Jareth to one side of her, the Sheik with his dark, rapacious eyes sitting opposite.

The next hour was a blur; she was hardly aware of what she was eating, didn't taste the hot, sweet tea or feel the water that was poured over her fingers at the beginning and the end of the meal. Jareth kept up a smooth flow of light, easy conversation, and after a while Sophie realised that he was trying to distract the Sheik's attention from her. She was uncomfortably aware of that heavy black gaze fixed on her almost obsessively throughout the meal, though, and although the Sheik answered Jareth's questions courteously, it was clear that his mind was elsewhere. Tense undercurrents shimmered between the two men, Jareth cool and controlled, the Sheik almost feverish underneath the civilised façade he had adopted for the meal.

When the interminable meal was finally over, Jareth skilfully brought the conversation to a close, then glanced at his watch.

'It's getting late and I believe my wife is tired,' he said. 'Perhaps one of your men could show us to the tent which you've kindly made ready for us?'

Although it was very obvious that the Sheik was loath to let Sophie leave, he finally got to his feet and clapped his hands. As Ahmed entered, he gave him instructions in swift Arabic, then he turned back to his guests.

'Ahmed will take you to your tent. I hope you sleep well. We will meet again in the morning, when there are one or two things I wish to discuss with you.'

Sophie stumbled wearily out of the tent, Jareth's hand clasped under her arm to keep her steady. It was such a relief to be free of the Sheik's piercing, lascivious gaze that she released a deep sigh and ran her fingers over her damp forehead.

As they followed the tall figure of Ahmed, she glanced up at Jareth.

'Why on earth did you agree to stay the night?' she asked, a trifle indignantly. 'All I want is to get away from this place—and that horrible man!'

'Keep your voice down,' Jareth warned quietly. 'Ahmed may understand English. And as to why I agreed to stay—the Sheik never intended to give us any choice. If we hadn't stayed voluntarily, he'd have found other, far less pleasant ways of keeping us here.'

Her eyes opened wide.

'But he can't do that——!' she began.

'Of course he can,' Jareth interrupted grimly. He gestured to the empty desert all around them. 'Who's to stop him? We're miles from any kind of official authority. And as far as the Sheik's men are concerned, his word is law. They'll do whatever he orders them to do.'

Sophie gulped.

'I've got us into a lot of trouble, haven't I?' she whispered.

'Yes, you damned well have,' he answered bluntly, and she couldn't say anything more after that, her throat seemed to have closed up completely. Instead, she trailed along miserably after Jareth, towards a small tent that was set a little apart from the others.

Inside, she could just make out a low bed of wooden laths bound together with strips of hide, while their own possessions had been neatly stacked in one corner. After Ahmed had left them, Jareth reached into his saddlebag and took out a small battery-operated lantern which, when switched on, filled the tent with a soft, pale glow.

'Right,' he said tersely, no trace of the lover in his voice now, 'I think it's time for some explanations.'

'You're angry with me, aren't you?' muttered Sophie dolefully.

For a moment she thought he was going to explode. She actually flinched as she saw the storm clouds gathering in his eyes. Then she relaxed again just a fraction as she saw him make a tremendous effort to keep his temper under control.

'You're fond of understatements, aren't you?' he said tightly. 'Yes, I'm angry. I think I've every right to be, don't you? You've got us into one hell of a mess and right now I don't know how we're going to get out of it. You're not blind, you saw the way Sheik Rashid looked at you. He *wants* you. And he's a man who's used to getting what he wants,' he added forcefully. 'Do you understand what I'm saying, your ladyship? The adventure's over, the games have stopped. This is reality, and you're not going to find it very pleasant.'

He tossed a blanket on to the bed, sat down and stared ahead broodingly. Sophie sank into a small, crumpled heap at his feet, twisted her fingers together nervously and wondered who she was more scared of at the moment, the Sheik or Jareth Kingsley.

'Can't we just creep away?' she suggested nervously.

'And do you think the Sheik's men are going to let us just walk out of here, when the Sheik's given orders that we're to stay?' came his sardonic reply.

'I was only trying to be helpful,' she muttered a little resentfully.

At that, the blue eyes flared into life and the tightly suppressed temper finally broke free of all the restraints he'd put on it.

'Helpful!' he repeated furiously. 'You run off, stumble straight into the hands of some sex-mad sheik, drag us both into the most appalling danger—and you call that being helpful?'

'I didn't want to go with those nomads in the first place, you know I didn't,' Sophie retorted spiritedly. 'It's really all *your* fault for being such a bully, making me do something I didn't want to do——'

Her small burst of rebellion swiftly died away as she saw the expression on his face. For the first time in her life, she was truly terrified of another human being. Then he must have seen the fear in her eyes, because he ran his hands tiredly through his thick, silky hair, shaking his head in defeat.

'Don't worry, I'm not going to hit you,' he said wearily. 'I've done a lot of things in my life that I'm not particularly proud of, but I've never yet hit a woman and I'm not about to start now, even though you'd try the patience of a saint.' He drew in a deep breath, seemed to reach a decision. 'Look, right from the beginning we've been at each other's throats. It's probably as much my fault as yours——'

'Oh, it's very good of you to admit that,' she interrupted haughtily.

'Don't keep deliberately riling me, Sophie,' he growled. 'You're just making this much harder for both of us.'

'Sorry,' she muttered contritely. 'It's just that I'm scared to death, and it's making me prickly.'

'It's all right, I understand,' he said with unexpected discernment. 'How about a truce, even if it is only temporary? We'll stand a much better chance of getting out of this mess if we're not at each other's throats all the time.'

'Okay,' she agreed in a subdued tone, after a moment's hesitation. Then she added curiously, 'How on earth did you find me? I nearly died when you turned up in the Sheik's tent!'

'So did the Sheik,' he commented dryly. 'He wasn't expecting your husband to burst in halfway through his seduction scene.'

Sophie giggled.

'That was a piece of inspiration, pretending to be my husband,' she said, still grinning as she remembered the expression of sheer frustration on the Sheik's face. 'But how did you manage to turn up at just the right moment?'

'A couple of hours after I left you with the nomads, I had an attack of conscience,' Jareth admitted. 'I decided I'd better turn back, try and catch up with you, make sure you were all right. What I didn't expect,' he added with some acerbity, 'was to find you only a couple of miles or so behind me, being led off into the desert by a couple of cut-throats. I was frightened to tackle them in case you got hurt, so I decided the best policy was to follow you, see where they were taking you.'

'And here we both are,' she said lightly. 'Guests of the Sheik—whether we want to be or not.'

A frown crossed his face.

'Don't joke about this, Sophie,' he warned. 'There's nothing funny about the position we're in. I told you, Sheik Rashid's a man who's used to getting exactly what he wants. It's that damned hair of yours,' he added broodingly. 'He couldn't take his eyes off it all evening, it's like a magnet, he can't wait to run his hands through it, twist it round his fingers, feel its silkiness——'

He broke off abruptly, as if he hadn't meant to say so much.

Sophie stared at him worriedly, not hearing the sudden roughening of his voice.

'But what can I do about it?' she asked, fingering the long, apricot-coloured plait absently. 'It's no use hiding it, he's already seen it. I can't see what would help, short of cutting if off——'

Her voice trailed away and she felt herself go pale.

'Oh no,' she pleaded softly, 'you don't want me to do that, do you? David loves my hair, he'd be devastated if I turned up with it chopped short!'

For some reason, that seemed to anger him. A faint flare of colour showed along his high cheekbones.

'Does he love you or your hair?' he demanded. 'If he's just like Sheik Rashid, a man obsessed with long blonde hair, then perhaps you ought to think twice about marrying him.'

How dared he say such things! Sophie glared at Jareth angrily. Of course, a man like him would never understand someone like David, who loved the beautiful, the delicate things of life. He loved her hair in the same way that he loved a painting or a piece of music. He was a man of very high sensitivity, she reminded herself, with a small toss of her head.

'Of course David loves me!' she declared staunchly. 'It's just that he prefers my hair the way it is—and so do I.'

'If your hair means more to you than your life, then by all means hang on to it,' he commented with some exasperation. Then, seeing her stricken face, he added more gently, 'All right, calm down, there's no need to get melodramatic. We're not in any immediate danger just yet. Let's put it aside as an option to be considered later, if things get dramatically worse.'

She let her gaze drift up to his.

'Do you think that's likely to happen?' she asked in a low voice, suddenly very subdued.

'My guess is that Sheik Rashid's a very quick-tempered, hot-blooded, unpredictable man,' Jareth told her bluntly. 'It would be as well to be prepared for anything.' He reached over for another blanket and spread it on the low bed. 'There's not much we can do right now, though. It would probably be best to grab a couple of hours' sleep, while we can.'

'I couldn't possibly sleep——' began Sophie, then she realised that she certainly could; she was dog-tired, all the fraught events of the day beginning to catch up with her.

Wearily she clambered on to the bed.

'I wish I could have a bath,' she murmured wistfully.

'You smell very nice—very female,' he answered almost absently.

Suddenly too tired to answer, Sophie drew the blanket up around her shoulders and was about to snuggle down when she realised that Jareth hadn't moved off the bed.

A flicker of suspicion flashed through her.

'Where are *you* going to sleep?' she demanded.

'Right here, on this bed,' he replied calmly.

At that, her eyes shot open.

'You can't!' she retorted. 'It's—it's too small,' she finished slightly desperately.

'It'll take two people quite comfortably if we curl up close,' he said practically.

She sat up, dragging the blanket tighter around her shoulders.

'If you were a gentleman, you'd sleep on the floor!' she told him furiously.

'But I'm *not* a gentleman,' he reminded her silkily. 'And since the floor's cold and hard, I've certainly no intention of sleeping on it tonight.'

'Then I'll sleep on it,' she announced, flouncing off the bed and moving as far away from it as she could get.

'As your ladyship wishes,' he drawled, with an infuriating note of amusement in his voice.

And with that, he turned out the lamp.

He was right, the floor was incredibly hard, and the chill of the night seemed to be seeping right up through it, into the very marrow of her bones. No matter which way she lay, she couldn't get comfortable, and it was pretty obvious she wasn't going to get a wink of sleep like this.

After half an hour she sat up and glared into the darkness.

'Are you still awake?' she hissed.

There was no reply, just the sound of light, steady breathing.

For another five minutes Sophie sat there and shivered, getting colder and stiffer, tussling with her principles. Then she let out an exasperated sigh, clambered to her feet and groped her way over to the other side of the tent.

She finally found the bed by the simple process of walking straight into it. A rude word escaped her as she knocked her leg hard on the wooden frame, and she heard a small tut of disapproval drift out of the darkness.

'A most unladylike thing to say,' Jareth reproved softly. 'Do I take it that you're willing to risk unknown dangers by sharing this bed with me?'

'It looks like it's the only way I'm ever going to get a wink of sleep,' she said sulkily, then added accusingly, 'one thing's for certain, David would never treat me like this, behave so badly.'

'But David's a paragon of virtue, isn't he?' purred Jareth. 'The trouble is, he also sounds extremely boring.'

'David is *not* boring,' she insisted, almost tearfully. 'Why do you keep saying such horrible things about him when you don't even know him?'

'Perhaps I'm getting a little tired of hearing how saintly David is,' he yawned. 'Are you coming to bed or not? I want to go back to sleep.'

Gingerly she crept in beside him, and was immediately horrified at how little room there was. The only way the two of them could fit on it comfortably was for Jareth to mould the shape of his body to her own, his chest against her back, thighs pressing against the back of her knees. It was—well, unsettling, she admitted with a small gulp, trying to ignore the steady warmth that flowed from him, the faint echo of his heartbeat echoing through her own body.

He slid his arm around her waist and she instantly tensed.

'Don't worry, I'm not about to demand to have my wicked way with you,' he teased sleepily. 'It's just more comfortable this way.'

'It might be for you, but I'm certainly not comfortable,' Sophie grumbled, nervousness making her voice slightly shrill.

He shifted slightly and as his thigh moved nearer hers, she perceptibly jumped, all her nerve-ends constricting instinctively.

'Oh, hell, this is ridiculous!' he said impatiently, his good mood swiftly vanishing. 'Let's get one thing straight or neither of us are going to get a wink of sleep. I have not—*not*—got any designs on your virtue. If you're still a virgin—and I rather suspect you are, my lady, despite all those sophisticated airs you like to put on—you'll be able to embark on your wedding night with a clear conscience. I certainly won't have put the proverbial stain on your character.'

'How do I know I can trust you?' she demanded. 'Come to think of it, I don't know a single thing about you, you're a perfect stranger. I've no idea who you really are, what you're doing here, wandering around the desert all by yourself. You're a pretty mysterious character, Jareth Kingsley.'

He sighed softly.

'Do you always talk this much in bed? If you do, I'm actually starting to feel rather sorry for David, he's going to have a pretty frustrating honeymoon.'

Sophie flung herself round to face him.

'If you make one more snide remark about David——'

Even in the darkness she could see the warning glint of his eyes.

'Be careful about threatening me,' he said in a cool voice, 'or I might be tempted to tell David about how we shared a bed. And I don't think he'd be very pleased to hear about that, do you, your ladyship?'

She went quite cold.

'You wouldn't——' she whispered.

'I might,' he warned. 'And now, if it'll shut you up and let us both get some sleep, I'll tell you a few straight facts about myself, and hope to God it finally satisfies your insatiable curiosity for prying into other people's lives. My name really is Jareth Kingsley, I'm thirty-five years old, and I originally trained as an engineer, although I'm now involved more in electronics. As to what I'm doing here——' He hesitated, and she had the impression he was suddenly reluctant to go on. After a brief pause, he eventually began talking again, though. 'A few months ago, I was involved in a bad accident. It—made me look at life in a rather different way, changed something inside me.'

'The accident—was that when you hurt your leg?' she asked directly. 'I noticed that you limp rather badly.'

'You don't believe in phrasing things tactfully, do you?' he commented wryly. 'Yes, I did hurt my leg in the accident, but more than that, I got messed up inside my head. I needed—well, I needed to get away from everything, from everyone for a while.'

'But why here? Why the desert?'

She felt him give a small shrug.

'I didn't head for here straightaway. I wandered around Europe for a while, but it seemed too crowded, I kept bumping into people I knew. I'd been here once before, several years ago. I was involved as chief engineer on a big project organised by one of the major charities to sink a series of new wells in an area that had been hit by drought. There was something about the wildness and desolation of the land, the hospitality and the pride of the people who somehow managed to survive here in these harsh conditions, that strongly appealed to me. So I finally headed back here. I suppose I knew this was the one place on earth I'd be able to find the peace I needed.'

'Until I turned up,' remarked Sophie slightly ruefully.

'Until you turned up,' he agreed, and yet he didn't sound particularly angry any more.

'What about your family?' she prompted. 'You

haven't said a word about them.'

'And I don't intend to,' he told her equably. 'I've answered more than enough questions for tonight. For heaven's sake, stop chatting and *go to sleep*!'

Sophie wriggled a little further under the blanket, trying hard to get comfortable on the narrow bed. Somehow, though, she ended up lying even closer to him than before, so close, in fact, that she could feel the imprint of his body from head to toe, making her flushed with a mixture of embarrassment and a strange tingly heat that she was terrified he would be able to detect.

'Sorry,' she muttered, trying to squirm away from him, leave a small gap between them.

The warm breath from his exasperated sigh brushed the nape of her neck.

'Perhaps this is a good time to tell you one more fact about myself,' he said, no trace of expression in his voice now at all. 'That accident didn't just leave me with a limp. It knocked all the usual physical responses right out of me. *All* the responses. Do you understand what I'm saying? For the last few months I haven't had the slightest desire to touch any woman, and you're no exception. You're as safe in this bed with me as you would be in your own bed at home.'

His announcement completely flattened her, it was the very last thing on earth she would ever have expected to hear him say.

'You don't mean——?' she croaked, horror clear in her voice.

'Oh, don't worry, nothing's physically missing,' he answered in a sardonic tone. 'It's just a mental block, the desire simply isn't there any more.' She felt him give a small shrug. 'It isn't particularly important. It'll probably sort itself in time.'

'Can't you get help?' she said in a small voice.

'That psychiatrist you recommended once before?' he said drily. 'No, thanks, my head might be messed up, but I prefer to sort it out on my own, I don't need anyone else poking around inside it.'

'If you're doing so well on your own, why are you wandering around all by yourself in the desert, afraid to go home?' she questioned perceptively.

A small growl sounded in his throat.

'I never said I was afraid to go home!'

'You're still here,' she pointed out.

'Heaven save me from amateur psychologists!' he breathed. 'I only told you all this so you'd stop wriggling round the bed and let me get some rest. I thought it would make you feel more relaxed.'

'How can I relax when I'm worried about all the problems you've got?' Sophie demanded.

'They're *my* problems, not yours,' he told her a little curtly. 'The only thing you've got to worry about right now is what I'll do if I hear one more word from you tonight!'

'But——' she began.

'Sophie!'

There was something in his tone that finally shut her up. It was ages before she could get to sleep, though; his astounding confession kept echoing through her head, she could hardly believe it, yet she knew he wouldn't lie about something like that. What kind of accident could have caused such a traumatic after-effect? And how long was it going to go on affecting him? Weeks? Months? The rest of his life?

She finally dropped off, but it seemed as if she'd been asleep for only minutes when something woke her up again. Opening eyes that felt incredibly heavy, for a couple of seconds she could not remember where she was. Then she heard a low moan in her ear and realised that it was Jareth who had awakened her, tossing about restlessly beside her, muttering feverishly under his breath, finally striking out wildly with one arm, as if trying to push something violently away from him.

Only just ducking his flailing hand, Sophie raised herself up on one elbow and dug him hard in the ribs to try and wake him.

'Jareth, you're having another bad dream,' she said a little crossly. Really, this was too much! Two nights running she'd been woken by his nightmares, she was getting really fed up with this.

She poked him even harder, felt him stir in the darkness, saw the pale glitter of his eyes as he at last dragged them open.

Leaning over, she switched on the small battery operated lamp and saw by its dim light that his skin glistened with sweat, the blue eyes were still slightly out of focus.

'Just how often do you get these dreams?' she demanded.

'I haven't had them for several weeks,' he responded, with a small shudder. 'I thought I'd finally managed to get rid of them. Something must have triggered them off again.'

'I suppose you're going to blame that on me, too,' she sniffed.

'You're not exactly the sympathetic type, are you?' he said tiredly, sitting up and brushing his damp hair back from his face.

At that, Sophie softened.

'I thought you'd probably be utterly sick of sympathy,' she said honestly. 'I remember an accident I had a couple of years back, I slipped on some ice and broke my arm. For the first few days it was lovely, having everyone fussing round me. By the end of the week, it was beginning to grate a little, and soon it nearly drove me right up the wall, I felt as if I were being suffocated. I thought perhaps *you* were beginning to feel that way, too, that that was why you wanted to get right away from everyone.'

Jareth ran a slightly shaky hand over his forehead.

'I was running away from rather more than sympathy,' he admitted in a low voice. 'What I was trying to run away from was my own guilt. You can't do it, though. No matter where you go, how fast you travel, it races right alongside you all the time, it's always damned well *there*.'

'But why on earth do you feel guilty?' she asked, puzzled. Then her face became shadowed. 'Was there someone else involved in the accident?' she questioned him quietly. 'What was it, a car smash-up? Were they——' she chewed her lip anxiously, 'were they badly hurt?'

For a long time she didn't think he was going to answer. Then the words poured out of him, as if they'd been held back for so long that they simply refused to be held in check one second longer.

'Not a car, but a plane,' came his unsteady confession. 'A light plane, a four-seater—I was the pilot. So stupid, really, a joy-ride, I didn't even want to go. But this girl I'd been going out with for a few weeks talked me into it and she brought along another couple to make up a foursome. Such a shallow, spoilt girl, her father owned half the county, he'd given her everything she'd ever wanted since the day she was born. I was already tired of her, I knew I didn't want to see her again. I suppose that agreeing to the joy-ride was a way of softening the blow.' He hesitated, the dark blue eyes almost black now with self-imposed torment. 'The engine cut out about quarter of an hour after we took off. I don't remember much of it, it all happened so fast. The others were panicking, screaming—I tried everything I knew to keep control of that plane, but it was just no damned good, I couldn't keep it in the air——'

In the semi-darkness of the tent, Sophie shared his horror, his rackingly vivid memories of those terrifying moments. Her hand stole out, rested on his tense fingers, although he didn't even seem to feel her comforting touch.

'When we crashed, it was like the world coming to an end,' he muttered hoarsely. 'The noise, the confusion, everything ripping to bits all around me—then a terrible silence, the most dreadful silence you could imagine.' He turned to face her, his gaze burning bright now, his mouth set in a grim, hard line. 'Do you know why it was so silent?' he challenged bitterly.

Numbly, she shook her head.

'Because I was the only one left alive!' As her heart twisted with awful pity, she saw the anger flare up inside him, making him shake with its force.

'I was the pilot, I was responsible, *I* was the one who should have died! Instead, I was the only one carried out alive. Oh, there was an official inquiry, I was completely cleared of all blame, they said no one could have prevented the crash. It makes no difference to the way I feel inside, though, it doesn't get rid of all the damned guilt. Three people died because of me—and I feel as though I murdered them!'

CHAPTER FOUR

THERE was no more sleep for either of them after that. Jareth sat hunched on the edge of the bed, while Sophie twisted her fingers together and wildly tried to think of some way to help him, to exorcise the ghosts that haunted him.

In the end, he shrugged broodingly.

'There's no point in spending the rest of the night dwelling on the past,' he said. 'We've got enough problems facing us right now without digging up even more.'

'Often it's a good thing to talk about your hang-ups,' she said quietly.

'I've managed perfectly well so far by keeping them to myself,' came his sharp retort. 'God knows what made me bore you to death with them tonight.'

At that, her head shot up and she fixed her velvet brown gaze directly on him.

'I was not bored, you know that perfectly well. And at least I'm starting to understand now why you're often so bad-tempered, so overbearing.'

'Am I really all those things?' he frowned, looking genuinely surprised. 'I don't mean to be.'

Sophie wrinkled her nose reflectively.

'I was beginning to think it was just me, that you couldn't stand being near me,' she said with complete honesty. Then she frowned slightly, and added, 'Perhaps it *is* me. Maybe I just bring out the worst in you. I mean, I don't want to pry, but that girl who talked you into taking them up in that plane—she sounds rather

67

like the spoilt society brat that you're always accusing me of being. Perhaps I remind you of her——'

As her voice trailed hesitantly away, he firmly shook his head.

'You're absolutely nothing like her. Yes, you're spoilt,' he added frankly, 'and you're self-willed, and you irritate the hell out of me at times, but you're certainly not shallow or empty-headed.'

She regarded him suspiciously.

'I'm not sure if that's a compliment or not.'

'Don't let's waste time arguing about it. Our main problem right now is Sheik Rashid and the fact that he wants to take you to bed. Unfortunately, all the advantages are on his side. If I can't somehow get you out of here, chances are that he's going to do precisely what he wants.'

To her annoyance, Sophie found herself flushing at his bluntness. As he saw the sudden wave of colour, he raised one dark eyebrow in faint surprise.

'I thought you were a girl who approved of plain speaking? Don't go all prissy on me, Sophie, this is a situation that's got to be faced up to and dealt with or we're both going to be in a lot of trouble.'

'It's just that that man gives me the creeps,' she said with a small shiver of revulsion. 'He looks as if he knows every single thing a man can do to a woman, as if he's actually *done* every one of those things.'

'I'm not exactly inexperienced myself,' admitted Jareth drily. 'In fact, before the accident I had a track record that I'm not particularly proud of, looking back on it. Does that mean you put me in the same category as the Sheik?'

'Of course not!' Her response was immediate, instinctive. 'No, definitely not,' she repeated again. 'You—well,' she went on a trifle awkwardly, 'I think you'd make love to a woman, really make *love* to her, you know what I mean? While the Sheik, he'd just use her, he'd only be interested in his own pleasure, he wouldn't care a fig what she felt, what she needed——'

Her voice trailed away in utter embarrassment as she realised she'd blurted out far more than she'd intended.

'Thanks for the character reference,' said Jareth with an unexpected grin. Then he frowned again. 'Now, how to get out of here?' he went on thoughtfully. He was silent for a couple of minutes, then glanced over at her. 'Have you got any money left?'

'Money?' she echoed. 'Yes, of course. I spent some of it buying that camel from the nomads, but I've still got quite a bit.'

She rummaged in her bundle for her purse, then pulled out a large wad of notes and tossed them over to him. Jareth released a silent whistle as he swiftly counted it.

'Carrying this much around, you were lucky not to be robbed. How much of it can you afford to give away?'

Sophie shrugged casually.

'Take all of it, if you want.'

He took out his own wallet, added a handful of notes to her own, then got to his feet.

'With luck, there'll only be one guard posted. This is obviously the Sheik's own territory, he probably feels pretty safe here. There's only one way we're ever going to get out of here, and that's to try and bribe the guard to turn a blind eye.'

She looked at him doubtfully.

'Will it work?'

'I don't know,' he admitted. 'These men are all in awe of the Sheik, it's going to take a lot of money to make one of them deliberately disobey the Sheik's orders.'

'You've got a lot of money,' she pointed out a little

tartly. 'I've just given you a small fortune.'

'It's *your* neck I'm trying to save,' he reminded her. 'Or rather, your virtue. Or had you forgotten that?'

No, she hadn't forgotten. In fact, she could almost see the Sheik's lustful eyes in front of her right now, as if he were actually in the tent with them. As Jareth slipped out of the tent, she fervently prayed he would be successful in his attempt to bribe the guard.

It seemed ages before he came back. Without saying anything, he swiftly began to gather together their belongings.

'He took the bribe?' she breathed.

'Luckily, yes. His eyes nearly popped out, I shouldn't think he's ever seen so much money in his life before. Evidently the Sheik expects them to stay with him through loyalty, not because he pays them well.'

'Won't he get into trouble?' asked Sophie worriedly. 'I mean, when the Sheik wakes up in the morning and finds we've gone, he isn't going to be too pleased, is he?'

'I think that's something of an understatement,' remarked Jareth a little grimly. 'My guess is that the guard won't be around, either. He'll have skipped off to somewhere where he can spend his money. Now get moving—the bigger head start we've got, the safer we'll be.'

Clutching her bundle of possessions in one hand and gripping Jareth's fingers with the other, Sophie let him lead her out into the darkness. Silently, they threaded their way past the other tents, to where their camels were waiting. There was no sign of the guard, and a couple of minutes later they were mounted and heading the camels away from the Sheik's camp.

Once they had gone some distance and their voices would no longer carry back to the sleeping Arabs, Jareth turned to her.

'We'll make our way back to the main trail, then follow it until it becomes light. It would be madness to try and make our way over rough country at night, we'd soon get hopelessly lost. In the morning, though, we'll have to try and get off the beaten track. The Sheik may well send some of his men after us.'

Alarm oozed out of every one of Sophie's pores.

'Surely he wouldn't do that?' she protested. 'He can't want me *that* much?'

'You saw the look in his eyes as well as I did,' he reminded her grimly. 'My guess is that he's become obsessed with you. And a man like the Sheik's capable of almost anything once he's in the grip of a fever like that.'

Sophie edged her camel a little nearer to his.

'I'm glad you're here,' came her muttered confession. 'I think I'd have gone completely to pieces if I'd been on my own.'

'Then I'm obviously the ideal person to have around. If there's one thing I'm an authority on, it's going to pieces,' he replied with a touch of self-mockery. 'The trouble is, I'm not so good at putting all the pieces back together again.'

She refused to let him belittle what he'd done.

'No one else could have got me out of this mess,' she insisted.

One dark eyebrow quirked upwards.

'Not even the saintly David?'

And with that cutting reminder that she had no business staring at him with that faint glow of hero-worship in her eyes, Jareth urged his camel slightly ahead of hers, leaving her with a clear view of his uncompromisingly straight back.

Oh, why did he always have to spoil everything? Sophie sighed angrily. It was almost as if—well, almost

as if he were afraid of being too nice to her. Every time
the conversation slipped to a personal level, he would
suddenly pull back, say something to deliberately upset
her. But why did he bother? She was hardly any kind of
threat to his peace of mind. After all, he had already
made it painfully clear that his interest in the opposite
sex was at zero level at the moment, some kind of
psychological after-effect of that dreadful plane crash
that had so completely shattered him.

Tired of trying to fathom this mysterious man, she
concentrated instead on guiding her plodding camel
along in his wake. She might not understand Jareth
Kingsley, but for some odd reason she felt safe with
him, and so she intended to stick to him like glue.

They eventually reached the rough track she had been
riding along when the Sheik's men had first grabbed
her, then they followed it as it wound its way through
the bleak emptiness of the starlit desert. It was cold and
eerily silent, with the light from a nearly full moon
touching everything with a pale gilding of silver. They
travelled on steadily until the sky at last began to lose its
dark velvet texture and the stars slowly faded. Colours
began to emerge from a landscape that, only minutes
ago, had been grey and lifeless. A faint touch of orange,
a flicker of gold, a patch of muted red, and now the sky
was becoming streaked with blue and purple.

As the first glow from the rising sun touched them
with its brightness and its promise of warmth to chase
away the chill of the night, they stopped for a brief rest
and something to eat and drink. Jareth pulled a map out
of his saddlebag and studied it for a while, then he
shook his head.

'Maps are pretty useless in the desert,' he explained.
'The features marked on them can change so quickly.
Water-holes dry up and disappear, villages can be

abandoned almost overnight if the grazing runs out, even the physical landmarks can alter.'

'In other words, if we leave this track, we stand a good chance of getting completely lost,' Sophie commented philosophically.

'Something like that,' he admitted. 'But I know there's a water-hole north-east of here, several Arabs I've talked to have mentioned it, a couple even gave me directions on how to get there. Finding it will be a bit of a gamble, though. Are you willing to take that risk?'

'I'll follow you anywhere, as long as it means I don't fall back into the hands of Sheik Rashid,' she declared fervently.

He lifted one eyebrow in a familiar, sardonic gesture.

'I just hope your touching confidence in me isn't misplaced. All right, my lady, back on your camel and let's go in search of this elusive water-hole.'

It was funny, she mused, but she didn't really mind him calling her 'my lady' now. He somehow made it sound—well, almost like a term of affection.

Steady, Sophie, came that little warning voice at the back of her mind again. Don't get carried away just because he came galloping to your rescue like a knight on a white horse—or a camel, she added silently, giggling to herself at the mental picture that conjured up.

Then the grin died away and her delicate features grew serious again. Serious, and slightly wistful. Life had suddenly got so very complicated. It had all seemed so straightforward and easy back in England. Travel out, join David, get married, live happily ever after—a rather childish, fairytale-like dream, perhaps, but that was exactly how she'd pictured it happening.

Yet here she was, on the run from a lecherous sheik, her safety in the hands of a man who regarded her as nothing more than a nuisance.

A tiny sigh escaped her, as she stared gloomily at the man a few yards in front of her. A few hours ago in that tent, listening to his hoarse confession, she had felt extraordinarily close to him. Now he was a stranger again, as remote as during those few minutes when she had first opened her eyes and seen him, mistaken him for a bandit.

Why couldn't he be more like David? she frowned with a brief spurt of irritation. Uncomplicated, gentle, sensitive—just a little dull? As that treacherous thought slid sneakily into her mind, she gave a small gasp, then furiously pushed it away again. David most certainly wasn't dull, she told herself vehemently, of course he wasn't! He was the most wonderful man in the world and she was very, very lucky he wanted to marry her.

In an effort to remind herself how much she loved David, she tried to conjure up his face, but it stayed infuriatingly fuzzy and featureless. Oh, this was perfectly stupid, she knew exactly what he looked like, that soft, fair hair, his pale blue eyes, his rather sun-reddened skin. So why couldn't she put them all together, make a complete portrait in her mind that she could cling to, silently adore? David, where are you? she asked slightly desperately.

There was no answer, but she was far beyond the stage where she expected one. Something really funny was happening to her, she knew that now, although she couldn't work out what it was. She just clung doggedly to the thought that everything would be all right again when she was reunited with David, it *had* to be.

As the sun soared higher into the sky, then began to beat down with its full scorching heat, she pulled off her jumper and stared for a moment at her arms in fascination. The faint pattern of bruises was still clearly

visible around her wrists, the marks Jareth had left on
her skin after grabbing her while he was still caught in
the throes of that awful nightmare. It was as if she bore
his brand mark, they both bewitched and appalled her.
With an effort, she dragged her glazed eyes away from
them and tried to concentrate on the dusty trail ahead.

During the fiercest heat of the day, they rested in the
shade of a sprawling acacia tree. Although Jareth had
said nothing, Sophie knew that he was worried about
the small amount of water they had left. Although they
could survive without food for several days in this
pitiless land, without water they would be dead within
hours. They *had* to find that water-hole before sundown.

They travelled on through the afternoon, the lines on
Jareth's face becoming noticeably more marked as they
covered mile after dusty mile. Then Sophie's gaze fixed
on something in the far distance, something that
seemed to shimmer and dance in the heat, and she
caught her breath.

'Is that a reflection?' she whispered hopefully. 'Or am
I just seeing things?'

Jareth shaded his eyes, staring ahead for a couple of
minutes with tense concentration. Then the hard line of
his mouth relaxed into a shadow of a smile.

'It's the water-hole,' he said, with clear relief.

'I knew you'd find it!' she beamed at him delightedly.

He shot her a quizzical glance.

'Can you honestly swear that you weren't beginning
to have one or two doubts?' he challenged.

'Certainly not,' she lied stoutly. 'Come on, I'll race
you there!'

She coaxed her camel into a lumbering trot, and
heard Jareth's animal thudding along just behind her.
The hot breeze lifted the hair from her face, sent it
flying out behind her in a dazzling banner, and she

threw her head back in sheer delight.

'Slowcoach!' she tossed back at him provocatively, forgetting all the traumas of the last couple of days in this mad dash towards the water-hole.

'Spoilt brat!' he goaded in response as his camel drew level with hers, yet there was no malice in his voice, only a carefree teasing that completely astounded her; she'd never seen him like this before, in a mood that was almost playful.

She matched her own camel's pace to his own, and they tore across the last stretch of desert side by side, cheerfully yelling insults at each other. Jareth was marginally ahead by the time they reached the edge of the pool. He slid from the saddle, unloaded both camels, then led them down to the water for a well-deserved drink.

'Phew, I'm hot!' groaned Sophie, sinking down on to the sun-scorched ground.

'Why not take a swim?' he suggested.

Her eyes flew open hopefully.

'Do you really mean it?'

He shrugged.

'Why not? I'll just hobble the camels, then I'll join you. I could certainly do with a wash.'

Sophie began to undo the buttons of her blouse; then she involuntarily shot a rather nervous glance over her shoulder. To her relief, Jareth seemed fully occupied with the camels, who weren't in a particularly good mood after their sudden enforced dash across the desert. Rather hurriedly, she stripped off her blouse and jeans, then she stood there for a moment in her thin cotton bra and pants feeling ridiculously exposed.

Don't be such a prude, she lectured herself as she scurried down to the water's edge. There's absolutely no one to see you—well, no one except Jareth, and he's just not interested in women at the moment, he was pretty explicit on that point.

The water was deliciously cool against her heated skin. It glistened like glass in the late afternoon sunlight, and after washing the dust off her skin and out of her hair, she floated blissfully on her back, her gaze drifting over the soft, red hills in the distance, the acacia and palm trees that clustered round the water's edge, offering welcome patches of shade, and the pale, ivory sand. Then she watched a pair of black eagles gliding effortlessly overhead, etching endless patterns against the blue, blue sky. Closing her eyes, she released a faint sigh of pure contentment. Right now, this seemed as close to paradise as she was ever likely to get.

She opened her eyes again just in time to see Jareth walking down to the water's edge.

She'd seen him naked to the waist before, on that night he'd suffered the first nightmare and had had to change his sweat-soaked shirt. Now, though, he had stripped down to just a pair of cotton briefs, and to her embarrassment she just couldn't drag her gaze away from him.

The tawny-skinned body moved with a supple, almost sensual grace that she had only been able to dimly guess at before when it had been covered in the loose-fitting Arab clothes. He was a perfectly proportioned male animal, long-limbed, lean-hipped, flat-stomached, with an aura of leashed power that made her feel peculiarly weak. Wow! she whispered shakily. Views like this should be censored, they could keep a girl awake at night!

Then her gaze slid down further, to his deeply tanned legs, and the breath suddenly caught in her throat. She'd almost forgotten about his limp, he made so little of it that she hardly even noticed it any more. Those deep, vivid scars couldn't be ignored, though, they were etched so clearly into his skin that she knew he would bear them until the day he died. And for the first time, she began to have a vague inkling of the true extent of his injuries, what pain he must have gone through since the plane crash, the struggle it must have been even to walk again. So his suffering hadn't all been mental, it had been physical as well. No wonder it had just about torn him apart!

Yet as he reached the deeper water and swam out towards her, he seemed more relaxed than she had ever seen him before. His wet hair glistened blackly, the dark blue eyes were laughing as he surfaced beside her, tweaking her own long hair playfully.

'God, how marvellous to feel clean,' he said with some feeling.

'Pretty fantastic, isn't it?' Sophie agreed cheerfully, her own sombre mood lifting. 'That sand and dust works its way into the most extraordinary places!'

For a while they swam up and down lazily, working some of the stiffness out of their limbs after the long camel-ride. Then they floated companionably side by side, not speaking, simply relaxing after the exhausting events of the last twenty-four hours.

By mutual consent, they eventually made their way back towards the shore, trudging up the crusty terraces of sand towards the small grove of trees where they had left their bundles of possessions and equipment. Spreading a blanket out on the ground, they flopped down side by side in the fading heat of the sun.

'I've got a towel somewhere in my saddlebag,' murmured Sophie sleepily.

Jareth's fingers trailed lightly over her skin.

'You're almost dry already.'

Her eyes had been closed, but something in his tone

of voice made her open them again, and glance up at him sharply. He was lying beside her, propped up on one elbow, and for once the dark blue eyes weren't cool at all, there were strange little flames dancing in their depths, like the first flickerings of a firestorm.

Yet he wasn't looking at her face, instead his gaze had been drawn irresistibly downwards, as if dragged there by a force he couldn't control. Slightly nervously, Sophie glanced down at her own body, gulping with sheer embarrassment as she realised that her wet cotton bra was now clinging to her like a second skin, with the dark shadow of her nipples showing clearly through the thin material.

The sensible thing would be to turn over on to her stomach right now, before this went any further. Or better still, get dressed. But somehow she just couldn't move, in fact it was hard even to breathe. And worse still, her nipples were beginning to harden, the tiny stiff peaks pushing betrayingly against the damp cotton so that no one could miss their instinctive response.

One long, tanned finger moved slowly, inexorably, towards the nearest throbbing tip and lightly touched it, causing her to make a small, strangled sound in her throat. Then Jareth's dark head was moving, bending over her, his tongue moved in that same gentle, excruciatingly pleasurable caress, and she closed her eyes very tight, sure she must be dreaming.

He isn't interested in making love! she reminded herself wildly. He isn't interested, he told you that only last night, confessed that he'd had all the desire knocked out of him by the awful aftermath of that plane crash. This just can't be happening ...

Only those clever hands were moving again now, she could feel the front catch of her bra being unfastened, then the last rays of the setting sun were warming her bare flesh, only she didn't need warming, she was already burning hot, her body sending out wave after wave of heat.

His warm palm closed over the full swell of her flesh, gently massaging the softness as if reminding himself of the feel, the gloriously sensual shape of the female body. You're just a guinea-pig, Sophie, she told herself with a slightly sick feeling. He's testing his reactions, that's all, trying to find out if he's cured yet of all that guilt, that mental block that left him impotent.

Yet still she couldn't move. Her head was telling her one thing, but her traitorous body had suddenly developed a mind of its own, it was loving that gentle, rhythmic stroking, almost purring like a cat as his hand stole softly down her ribs and slid in tiny circles over her shuddering stomach.

I wish he'd kiss me!

The thought crept, unbidden, into her mind, shocked her with the intensity of need that lay behind it.

But his lips never touched hers, although she knew his face was very close, she could feel his breath lightly brushing her tightly shut eyelids.

Then his hand became still, lying languorously against her stomach where it had finally come to rest. She felt his head droop down against her shoulder, his damp hair brushing the nape of her neck in a tickly, curiously pleasant sensation that sent tiny tendrils of pleasure curling through her. For long minutes she waited for those killingly potent caresses to begin again, but he didn't stir, his long fingers remained motionless, imprinting five tiny pools of heat against the skin of her stomach.

At last she forced herself to open her eyes and glanced cautiously sideways, quivering slightly with apprehension as she wondered what mood she would find him in, what they would say to each other after that melting exploration of her body.

Jareth was asleep, lying against her perfectly relaxed, quite motionless, for once untroubled by bad dreams.

Sophie felt strangely tired herself, all her limbs heavy, her eyelids flickering with fatigue. With an odd little sigh, she closed them, curled a little closer to the man beside her; then she, too, drifted into sleep.

When she woke up again, it was dusk, and the blanket had been wrapped protectively around her near-naked body. Still feeling slightly strange, she rubbed her eyes tiredly, blinking hard to try and clear the last of the sleepiness away.

When she at last sat up, clutching the blanket tightly around her bare shoulders, she discovered they no longer had the water-hole to themselves. On the far side were desert nomads, setting up camp for the night and bringing their herds of camels down to the water to drink. A little alarmed at the sight of so many strangers, she instinctively looked around for Jareth, then released a brief sigh of relief as she saw his tall figure striding towards her.

Then her gaze drifted involuntarily down to his strong, beautiful hands, and right then she was very relieved that the light was fading fast because it meant he couldn't see the bright splash of colour that burned on her cheeks.

On his own face there was absolutely no hint of what had passed between them earlier. He looked relaxed, alert, crisply efficient.

'You're awake?' he said. 'Good. We've been invited to dinner.'

'Invited to dinner?' Sophie echoed feebly. 'Who by?' Then she remembered the legendary hospitality of the people of the desert and gave a faint smile. 'Of course, the nomads. Well, I really don't have a thing to wear, but I don't suppose they'll mind too much if we don't dress formally.'

'I'll go and check the camels,' he said tactfully as she scrambled to her feet, clutching the blanket even tighter round her as she started to rummage through her crumpled bundle of clothes.

He didn't return until she was fully dressed, then they walked round to the nomadic encampment, where Sophie had a chance to practise her very basic Arabic as all the prolonged ritual greetings were gone through. The nomads treated them with a mixture of respect and much curiosity, and Sophie guessed that it was pretty rare for them to meet two English people who were travelling through the desert on camels.

She stared around her with fascination as they made their way through the ordered chaos of the camp. Most of the tents had already been erected, thick sheets of canvas hoisted over wooden frames. The camels which had been watered were being brought back and hobbled near to the tents, and their mournful moans and snorts joined with the bleating of the goats to form a constant background of noise. Fires had been lit, and by their bright, flickering light Sophie could see the dark shadows of the women as they moved quickly and efficiently about their tasks, fetching bedding, preparing meals or pounding spices in huge wooden mortars.

She and Jareth were taken to an area of rugs and canvas sheets a little distance from the tents. As they settled themselves around the fire, they were brought bowls of water flavoured with buttermilk, then a dish of *asida*, a sort of porridge made from sorghum flour, with gravy poured over the top. Sophie had eaten *asida* before when travelling with the camel-herders, it was the staple diet of the desert people. She dipped her fingers into the piping hot porridge, scooped up a portion, dunked it into the gravy and then popped it into her mouth.

After they had eaten, a couple of the men entertained them with musical poetry, their songs telling of the everyday events of their lives, of the desert, of their beautiful girls. When the songs were finished, Jareth began to talk to the men, and although her Arabic was too limited to let her follow the rapid conversation, Sophie had the impression that he was asking quite a lot of questions. And from the faint frown that slowly appeared on his face, she guessed that he didn't much like the answers they were giving him.

It was late when they finally walked back to their own campsite. When they reached it, she tugged at his sleeve.

'Is something the matter?' she asked, rather anxiously. 'What did those nomads tell you?'

At first she thought he wasn't going to answer her. Then he gave a slightly impatient shake of his head.

'I suppose you've a right to know,' he replied rather tersely. 'I asked them if anyone had stopped by asking questions—and the answer was yes. Earlier today, just a few miles south of here, a man asked them if they'd seen a girl with long hair the colour of the sun.'

Apprehension surged through her and left her visibly trembling.

'Sheik Rashid's still looking for me?' she said in a quavery voice.

'It looks like it,' agreed Jareth, with some annoyance. His tone warned her that his mood had darkened.

'It's not my fault,' she said defensively, nerves making her voice rather sharper than she'd intended. 'I didn't *want* the Sheik to get this ridiculous obsession about me.'

'If you'd stayed in England, where you belonged, none of this would ever have happened,' he growled irritably.

'I didn't want to stay in England,' she declared with fierce defiance. 'I wanted to be with David, I missed him so much, I couldn't bear being apart from him one day longer.'

And for some reason, that seemed to make him even more angry. As the moonlight beat down on the dark planes of his face, she could see the tense lines etched there, the threatening glitter of those extraordinary eyes.

'And exactly what did you miss?' he goaded unpleasantly. 'His brilliant conversation—or his kisses?' He was looming over her now, like a great black shadow that was about to swallow her up. 'And exactly *how* did he kiss you?' he went on, his voice abruptly changing, lowering several tones, taking on a new, husky note. 'Like this?'

Before she could turn her head away, his lips were drifting over hers, touching lightly, tantalisingly, and it was funny, but it *was* like being kissed by David, that soft, gentle touch that left her feeling warm and fluttery inside, sort of relaxed and yet faintly dissatisfied, as if there should have been something more. Yet David had respected her, she'd known that, he would never have forced himself on her, and she should have been pleased about that, not secretly, guiltily wished that he would sometimes be a litle more—well, demanding.

'Do you like that?' murmured Jareth. 'Is that how David's kisses felt?'

Slightly stunned by his nearness, his velvet voice, the bright stars that framed the powerful silhouette of his body, Sophie nodded slowly, almost dreamily.

'Then he's a fool,' responded Jareth with unexpected savagery. 'He should have kissed you like *this*.'

And the stars went out, blotted out of existence by the darkness that swept over her as she was torn apart by the kiss that followed. Ruthlessly, he plundered the softness of her mouth, explored it as if it belonged exclusively to him, his own private pleasure-ground. Flung into a world she hadn't even known existed, she reeled under the fierceness of his attack, and found, to her shame, that a flame of exultation was flaring up inside her, she was opening up to him with an abandonment that terrified her.

That gentle flutter inside her had become a roar, a torrent, it was knocking her flat, she didn't even have the strength to gasp for air. And all from the touch of those hard lips, because apart from one hand locked on to her shoulder, holding her prisoner, no other part of his body was in contact with hers. She didn't even dare think about what might have happened if it had been.

The long, blinding kiss at last came to an end, and she stared at him with shocked eyes, dimly realising that he was nearly as shaken as she was.

With a small growl, he flung himself away from her, paced away for several yards. Then he sank down to the ground, sitting with his back propped against a tree trunk, staring out at the lonely stretches of the desert beyond.

'You'd better get some sleep,' came his curt order. 'We'll be making another early start in the morning.'

Sophie swallowed hard, wished that she wasn't still stupidly shaking.

'W—what about you?' she stammered unsteadily. 'You need some sleep, too.'

Jareth didn't move, didn't even look at her.

'I'll keep watch for a while. It's not very likely that any of the Sheik's men will turn up this late at night, but it makes sense to take a few basic precautions.'

With trembling fingers, she picked up her blanket and retreated a safe distance away from him; then she curled up in a small ball and tried hard to sleep. It seemed hours before her eyes finally closed, though. Her lips ached, her body ached, something deep inside her ached. And all the time, even when she closed her eyes, she could see the dark silhouette of that isolated figure sitting there, silent, motionless, withdrawn.

Time after time, she nearly got up and went over to him. Yet something always stopped her, even though she wasn't sure what it was. Guilt, perhaps, because she was engaged to David? Because she knew perfectly well she shouldn't be tempting fate this way? Or was it just something unapproachable about that dark figure? All her instincts warned her that he didn't want company tonight—and most certainly not hers!

While she was still trying to sort out all the confusion inside her aching head, her tired eyes finally drooped shut and she tumbled into a restless sleep.

CHAPTER FIVE

IN the morning Sophie woke up to find that Jareth was already moving around purposefully, saddling up his camel. Then, to her alarm, she saw that her own camel was still grazing peacefully nearby, with no saddle on its back.

Sitting bolt upright, she stared at Jareth fearfully.

'Are you running out on me?' she gulped.

The blue gaze swivelled round to fix on her.

'Don't tempt me,' he grated, that underlying note of irritability back in his voice again, 'or I might just take you up on that suggestion.'

'Then where are you going? Wherever it is, you've no intention of taking me, have you?' she accused. 'You've only saddled up one camel.'

He finished fixing his saddle into place, then walked over to her. With a small twinge of unease she noted that his eyes were coolly remote again, his expression as unreadable as when she had first met him. It was as if he were deliberately distancing himself from her, denying that anything had happened between them last night.

'I'll only be gone for a few hours,' he told her. 'There's a small town just to the east of here, one of the nomads gave me directions on how to get there. I'll pick up a few things we need, and with luck I'll be back by midday.'

'You will come back? You promise?' Sophie said in a very small voice.

Surprise showed briefly on his face, followed by a brief flicker of anger.

'You think I'd just abandon you?' he challenged

tersely. 'Is that the kind of man you think I am?'

Embarrassment swept over her, and she lowered her thick lashes so that he couldn't see her eyes.

'No—it's just that—well, I know you don't want to be stuck with me, I'm just a liability, aren't I?' she muttered, with a touch of self-pity creeping into her voice.

'Yes, you are,' Jareth agreed with brutal frankness. 'But like it or not, I'm responsible for you, so you can stop feeling so sorry for yourself, I'm not about to walk out on you.'

'Can't I come with you?'

'You'll be much safer here. Chances are Sheik Rashid will have some of his men watching the roads, and I don't want to risk running into them.'

Knowing that he was impatient to be gone, Sophie bit back any further pleas for him to take her with him, somehow fighting back the panic as she watched him mount the camel, ride steadily away from her. She knew he would come back, of course he'd come back, but oh, it was so hard to just sit here and watch that tall figure gradually disappearing into the distance, being swallowed up by the vast emptiness of the desert. And what if he *didn't* return, if she sat here and waited and waited, but she never saw him again?

Don't be stupid, Sophie, she lectured herself fiercely. He promised he'd be back, and whatever else he might be, he's not a man who'd ever break his word. You can trust him, I know it, he'll look after you for as long as he thinks you're his responsibility.

Funny, really, she reflected with a wry grimace. She was at last beginning to realise that the whole point of this trip had been not just to be reunited with David, but to break away from the rather smothering love of her parents, to prove to herself that she could lead a useful, independent life. And yet here she was, relying on a man to get her out of this mess she'd landed herself in. Of course, she didn't really need him, she assured herself hurriedly, she'd have managed perfectly well on her own. Somehow she would have got away from Sheik Rashid and found her way to Hajjar and David. All the same, she couldn't quite suppress a small shiver as Jareth finally vanished from sight, and all of a sudden she felt a strange and painfully acute wave of homesickness.

What would her parents be doing now? Her mother would probably be pottering around in the rambling garden that was her pride and joy, and which she had planted with old-fashioned roses and cottage garden plants that contrasted beautifully with the grey stone walls of the huge old house that was far too large for them, but which her parents loved far too much to leave. And what would she be doing if she was at home? Perhaps getting ready to go out for lunch with one of her friends? Or maybe ringing round, finding people to make up a foursome for tennis? Or perhaps she'd be arranging to go and stay with her cousin Kate for a couple of weeks. Ever since Kate had got her own flat in London, Sophie had often popped down to stay for a few days. The two of them would do the rounds of the nightspots and theatres, sometimes on their own, but more often with a couple of Kate's endless supply of good-looking men in tow.

A trickle of sweat ran down Sophie's back, bringing her sharply back to the present. She glanced around and saw the ocean of amber sand, the craggy red teeth of the hills, the pool of water glistening like glass. And everywhere there was nothing except a frighteningly desolate emptiness. The nomads who had camped here last night had long since left, moving on to the next

water-hole with their herds of camels and goats, and it
would be nightfall before another group of desert people
moved in to water their animals and set up their tents.

The morning absolutely crawled by, and by midday
the first waves of panic were beginning to lap at her
nerve-ends. He'll be coming soon, she assured herself
slightly frantically. Any moment now she would see a
dark speck in the distance. Then it would get nearer and
nearer until she could clearly see the man himself, that
silky, dark hair, the tall, straight-backed body, those
blue eyes that could be so cool one moment, then flare
impatiently into life the next.

Only no matter how hard she stared, the horizon
remained empty, nothing stirred except the shimmering
waves of heat and a pair of eagles soaring high
overhead, riding the thermals of hot air pulsing up from
the burning land below.

When a distant figure did finally come into sight,
halfway through the afternoon, she didn't even see it
straightaway. By then, her eyes were blurred and sore
from staring into the dazzling sunlight, and her head
ached fiercely with the effort of fighting back the panic
that kept threatening to run riot and swallow her up.

By the time she eventually spotted the moving
silhouette, it was clearly identifiable as a single rider,
moving steadily towards the oasis. Relief made her
spring to her feet, and she had actually run a few yards
forward when alarm bells suddenly jangled loudly inside
her head.

What if it wasn't Jareth? What if it was one of Sheik
Rashid's men—or worse still, Sheik Rashid himself?

'I'm sure it's Jareth, I *know* it's Jareth,' she muttered,
peering anxiously at the camel and its rider as they drew
closer. Even dressed in the loose-fitting Arab clothes,
there was something so distinctive about the bearing of

the rider that she was sure she couldn't be wrong.

All the same, she waited until she could actually see that dark, familiar face before rushing to meet him.

'I thought you were never coming, that you'd gone off and left me,' she babbled with relief.

A frown instantly shadowed his features.

'I promised you that I'd come back,' he reminded her a little sharply.

'Yes, I know, but—oh, never mind, you're here now and that's all that matters,' Sophie said happily. 'It was so lonely without you, it seemed like you'd been gone for hours and hours——' It suddenly dawned on her that she'd said far more than she'd meant to, and she hurriedly shut up. Jareth was only half listening, though, he had already turned away and was unsaddling the camel.

'Did you manage to get everything you wanted?' she asked, glancing at the small bundle which he had already lifted off and set to one side.

He nodded.

'Most of it's for you.'

'For me?' she echoed in surprise. 'What is it?'

Take a look,' he invited.

She opened the bundle eagerly, then her face dropped, her nose wrinkling as she took out the crumpled cotton clothes. They were similar to what Jareth was wearing himself, a couple of long, loose shirts and two pairs of baggy cotton trousers.

'Thanks,' she said without much enthusiasm, 'but I think I'll stick to jeans and T-shirts, if you don't mind. I mean, Arab clothes look fine on you, but I don't think they're exactly my style.'

The blue gaze glittered warningly.

'But I *do* mind, I haven't ridden miles in this heat so you can turn your nose up at them because they're not the height of fashion. Go and put them on.'

Stubbornly, she stood her ground.

'But I don't want to.'

Jareth glanced up and one look at his face told her
that it definitely wouldn't be a good idea to disobey him
over this. All the same, she was getting a little tired of
being dictated to. If she didn't make a stand somewhere, he'd just keep riding roughshod all over her, and
she certainly didn't intend to let him get away with that.

'Give me one good reason why I should wear those
clothes,' she challenged.

He finished hobbling the camel, then he straightened
up and she gulped a little because she'd forgotten just
how tall he was, the unnerving habit he had of towering
over her and making her feel totally insignificant.

'I'll give you two reasons,' he told her smoothly.
'Firstly, you'll be far cooler and more comfortable. And
secondly, you'll be much less conspicuous. At the
moment, the combination of that hair and your
European clothes makes you stick out like a sore thumb.
Now that's fine if you're turned on by the thought of
Sheik Rashid dragging you off to some exotic desert
hideaway and keeping you there until he's tired of you.'
As Sophie visibly shuddered, his voice softened a little.
'On the other hand, if you want to reach David with
your virtue intact, I suggest you go and change right
now.'

Without further argument, she picked up the clothes
and was about to preserve the last few tatters of her
modesty by disappearing behind a nearby bush when
she suddenly came to a halt.

'But what about my hair?' she frowned. 'What am I
going to do about that?'

'Have a look inside that other small parcel,' Jareth
instructed.

With some trepidation, she opened it. Then her brows drew together in puzzlement as she saw the fine black powder inside.

'What on earth is it?'

'According to the man who sold it to me, when it's mixed with water it's a very effective hair-dye.'

Sophie felt her lower lip start to tremble.

'You want me to dye my hair black?' she somehow got out in a voice that was distinctly quavery.

'Given a choice between dyeing it and cutting it, I thought you'd prefer to dye it,' he told her.

Her fingers involuntarily stole to a glistening strand of her apricot hair.

'But—will it wash out again?' she asked with shaky apprehension.

'I don't know,' he answered perfectly honestly. 'It's a water-based dye, so a good hairdresser should be able to get it out for you, but I can't give any written guarantees.' As she still hesitated, he gave a slightly impatient shrug. 'Come on, Sophie, where's your common sense? That hair of yours is gorgeous, but it's like some damned beacon. If you don't do something to disguise it, Sheik Rashid's men will be able to spot you from miles away.'

For a moment, all she could think of was that he had said her hair was gorgeous. Then she stared at the packet of dye again, dithered indecisively for a few more seconds before finally releasing a deep mournful sigh.

'I suppose you're right,' she conceded very reluctantly. 'But it had better wash out,' she added warningly, shooting him a baleful glance.

'Go and get changed while I make up the dye,' he instructed, calmly ignoring her dark threat.

Sophie grabbed the cotton clothes, disappeared

behind the bush and began to strip off. A couple of minutes later she re-emerged with an even more woeful expression on her face.

'I look terrible,' she grumbled.

Jareth shot her a fleeting glance.

'You look fine.'

'No, I don't!' Angry tears began to glisten in her eyes and she stamped her foot. 'Look at me! They don't even fit. I feel like a—a walking jumble sale!'

'For heaven's sake,' he exploded, finally losing his own temper, 'what on earth does it matter what you look like? There's no one around to see you.'

'There's you——'

The words burst furiously out of her before she could stop them. Realising too late exactly what she'd said, she abruptly shut up, felt a revealing wave of heat scorch through her. Why on earth had she said such a stupid, *stupid* thing? She hadn't meant it, of course she hadn't, she'd just got so worked up that she'd said the first thing that had come into her head.

When she finally found the nerve to look at Jareth again, she saw the dark shadow of anger had gone from his face, he was merely looking thoughtful now.

'I know it's hard for you,' he conceded at last. 'I don't know much about your background, but it's pretty obvious you've led a fairly pampered life up until now. The last few days must have been quite a shock for you, having to get used to a way of life so utterly different from anything you've known before. To be honest, you've coped far better than I ever thought you would. If you're really serious about marrying this David of yours, though, you're going to have to make quite a few more adjustments. This is a hard, demanding land. There's no room for anything but the essentials, you use up most of your time and energy just trying to survive.'

Sophie's head snapped up.

'You don't think I can cope with it, do you?' she accused.

He looked at her steadily.

'I didn't say that. I'm simply trying to get it into that spoilt little head of yours that what you look like, what you're wearing, will probably be the very least of your problems, once you're married.'

She sniffed irritably.

'I wish you'd stop calling me spoilt. I'm getting thoroughly sick of it!'

The blue eyes went a shade darker.

'And what else should I call you?' Jareth shot back caustically. 'Here we are, being hunted by Sheik Rashid's gang of cut-throats, and what's the only thing that's worrying you? That your clothes aren't a perfect fit! For God's sake, Sophie, for once in your life try to get your priorities right!'

A sense of shame crept over her, forcing her to turn away so that he couldn't see her face. Damn the man for being right all the time! she thought furiously. Didn't *he* ever make any mistakes, put a foot wrong?

Then she remembered exactly what had driven him to this wilderness, the disaster that haunted his dreams, that had left him broken inside. In comparison, her own problems suddenly seemed so insignificant that she wondered how she'd even had the nerve to mention them.

'Is the hair dye ready?' she asked in a much more subdued tone.

Jareth gestured towards a wooden bowl filled with a gleaming black mixture.

'You're sure you want to do this?' he asked.

'I thought I wasn't being given any choice,' she answered broodingly, eyeing the dye with unease.

'We nearly always have a choice in everything we do,' came his unexpectedly quiet reply. 'It's just a pity that we can never see the ultimate consequences of those choices. It would stop us making so very many mistakes.'

She looked at him steadily, knowing at once what he was thinking about, the horrific tragedy that was never far from his mind.

'If you'd known that plane was going to crash, then of course you'd never have taken off,' she told him bluntly. 'But there was no way you could have known it was going to happen, so you've got to stop blaming yourself, feeling all this guilt for something that wasn't your fault.'

Jareth raised his head jerkily.

'And how do you suggest I do that?' he shot back harshly. 'Simply blot it from my memory, pretend it never happened?'

She drew in a shaky breath, seeming to feel his tension reach across and touch her own suddenly raw nerves.

'I don't know how you do it,' she admitted honestly. 'But I'm sure that running away isn't the answer. You told me just now to get my priorities right. Well, perhaps you ought to try and do the same. Work out what's really important to you and build on that, gradually get back to a normal life again. You can't spend the rest of your life wandering around the desert like a nomad. You're a clever man, Jareth. It's a terrible waste to leave all that intelligence unused, can't you see that?'

He regarded her coolly.

'Is the lecture finally over?' came his polite enquiry.

Sophie felt herself flush.

'Okay, so it's none of my business,' she said with a

touch of defiance. 'Well, you might have stopped caring about other people, but you're going to find it damned hard to stop people caring about *you*!'

His eyes took on a strange hue.

'And do you care about me, my little Sophie?' he asked in a smoky tone.

Thrown off balance, she turned her head away.

'Now you're teasing me,' she said slightly sulkily.

Since she wasn't looking at him, she didn't see his face change.

'Yes, I'm simply teasing,' he answered in an unexpectedly heavy voice. He seemed suddenly restless. 'If you're going to dye your hair, let's get on with it,' he added abruptly.

Sophie bent her head forward so that her hair hung suspended over the wooden bowl in a golden cloud. Then, with a tiny shudder, she leant further forward and watched in fascinated horror as the gleaming coils vanished into the foul-looking liquid.

'Get your hair nearer the bowl,' instructed Jareth, 'and I'll work the dye right up into the roots.'

Gritting her teeth, she did as he had instructed, and felt his fingers deftly working the black dye over the rest of her hair. She was glad he was helping, she didn't think she could have managed it all by herself; she was actually shaking as she saw the last of her lovely hair being swallowed up by that awful goo.

'Okay, that's it,' he announced a couple of minutes later. 'Just hold still while I wash off the surplus dye.'

He tipped a bowl of clear water over her head, then handed her a strip of rough cotton material.

'Towel-dry it with this, then just leave it to dry naturally in the sun.'

Shutting her eyes so that she wouldn't have to see the dull black strands, Sophie vigorously rubbed her hair, then wound the strip of cotton round her head, turban-style.

Jareth shot her an unexpectedly sympathetic look.

'You're going to have to look at it sooner or later,' he remarked.

With a tiny sigh she pulled off the makeshift turban, letting the damp strands of hair tumble around her shoulders. Then she reached into her bundle and pulled out a small hand-mirror. Almost fearfully, she lifted up the mirror and peered into it.

'It looks absolutely awful!' she moaned instantly. 'David's going to hate it!'

Jareth's features altered, tightened.

'If David really loves you, he won't care if you're completely bald as long as you reach him safely.'

Sophie stared at her reflection sadly.

'You're a man, you just don't understand,' she complained.

He whipped the mirror out of her hand and flung it several yards away. Stunned, she stared up at him, flinched at the hard anger she saw in his eyes.

'I'm getting awfully tired of your self-pity,' he stated grimly. 'All right, so your hair's a different colour from usual. So what? A lot of women change their hair colour every few weeks, just for kicks. It's no great tragedy to have black hair instead of blonde. Just be grateful that you're alive and healthy and beautiful!'

With that, he limped away, tension visibly vibrating right through his body. He went directly down to the water's edge, and Sophie sat and watched in frozen silence as he stripped off his loose clothes, muscles moving sleekly under the dark silk of his skin. Then he plunged swiftly into the water and began to swim very fast towards the centre of the pool as if physical exercise were some kind of safety valve for the volatile mixture of emotions that kept exploding out of control.

He kept swimming at the same fast, furious pace all the time she was drying her hair, up and down, up and down, until she grew almost dizzy watching him. It was nearly half an hour later before he finally left the water, pulling his clothes on without bothering to dry himself so that they clung damply to the lean lines of his body.

Sophie felt a quiver of trepidation as he walked towards her, then flung himself down just a couple of feet away, a look of brooding introspection on his face.

'This is all my fault, isn't it?' she said with sudden insight. 'I make you edgy, rub you up the wrong way.'

Jareth shook his head slightly impatiently.

'The fault's mine, not yours. I've been like this ever since the accident, not caring a damn about anything one moment, flying off the handle about some trivial little thing the next. I don't know why it keeps happening and it must be hell for everyone around me, but I just don't seem to have any control over it.'

'It's all right,' she assured him in a subdued tone, 'I'm a lot tougher than I look, I can cope with the odd bout of bad temper.'

Yet it wasn't all right, and the trouble was she didn't know why. In fact, right now she felt almost as confused and mixed-up as he was, and she didn't like it, not one little bit.

She glanced up and found he was staring at her. That made her feel even more nervous, and she chewed her bottom lip uneasily.

'What is it?' she asked at length.

'Your eyebrows,' he told her, with an unexpectedly wry smile. 'You've got black hair, but blonde eyebrows.'

'Oh,' she said, with an answering grin. 'Well, what do you suggest we do about it?'

'Come here, and I'll see if I can darken them with a little of the dye.'

She inched closer, sitting very still as he dipped his finger into the small puddle of dye left in the bottom of the bowl, then gently, carefully applied it to her thin, arched eyebrows. His touch was light but sure, and to her dismay she quivered as his fingertip drifted across her face.

'What is it?' he asked, surprised. 'There's no need to be nervous, I won't let the dye drip in your eyes, if that's what's worrying you.'

It wasn't, but she decided a little grimly that there was no need to let him know that. Instead, she sat like a statue as he finished applying the dye, frantically trying to quell that betraying tremor of her nerve-ends.

'Your lashes are rather pale,' he remarked, 'but I'm not going to risk dyeing them. I've no idea what this dye's made of, so I don't know if it could damage your eyes or not.'

'It doesn't matter,' Sophie responded quickly, 'I've got some mascara in my bag, I'll use that instead.'

To her astonishment, he threw back his head and laughed.

'Oh, Sophie,' he said at last, still grinning broadly, 'you're the only girl I know who could produce a stick of mascara in the middle of the desert! Just what else have you got tucked away in that bundle of yours?'

She instantly flushed and didn't answer. There was no need for him to know about the small package of delicate silk and lace underwear, the flimsy nightdress that she had packed specially for the hoped-for honeymoon with David.

'It's getting late,' she said, hurriedly getting to her feet. 'I'll see if I can find some wood for a fire.'

The sun was beginning to dip towards the horizon

now, there was obviously no point in trying to travel any further today. They would have to spend another night at the oasis, then start off again early the next morning. Already more desert people were beginning to arrive at the oasis with their herds of camels and goats, but they were setting up camp on the far side of the water-hole, leaving Jareth and Sophie's own small camp-site quiet and undisturbed.

After they had eaten, Sophie huddled a little closer to the fire, making the most of its heat as the night air took on its usual chill edge.

'Back at Sheik Rashid's camp, you said you were in electronics now,' she reminded him. 'What exactly do you do?'

'I started up my own company a few years back, Kingsley Electronics. I suppose I was lucky, I launched the company just when the hi-tech explosion was really taking off, and we've expanded fairly rapidly since then,' he told her. 'Our main line is computers, with all the accompanying software, but we also market an extensive range of small electronic gadgets for use in both the home and the office. Most of them are extremely useful, although some are just 'executive toys', electronic games for adults. We also do a range of children's toys, teaching machines that at the same time are great fun. The kids who use them think they're just playing games, but in fact they're learning something every time they switch them on.'

'Who designs the gadgets and toys?' she asked curiously.

'I design most of them myself,' he admitted.

'I thought so,' she said, with some satisfaction. 'I *knew* you were clever.' Then she frowned. 'But who's been running the company while you've been away?'

'A man called Brian Peters,' he told her. 'He's my

second-in-command. He's worked with me on most of
the new projects, he knows almost as much about them
as I do. He's quite capable of looking after things until I
get back.'

At that, she jerked her head up.

'Then you do intend to go back?' she questioned
alertly.

Jareth gave a non-committal shrug.

'Like you said, I can't spend the rest of my life
wandering around aimlessly.'

'But *when* are you going back?' she persisted.

He shot her a quick frown.

'Don't push it, Sophie,' he warned.

'But it's not just your work, it's your family,' she went
on stubbornly, ignoring the impatient glitter of those
penetrating eyes. 'Surely they're missing you, worrying
about you? What about——' She swallowed hard, tried
to keep her voice completely steady. 'What about your
wife?'

'I haven't got one. And no family worth talking
about, either,' he answered brutally.

Shocked, she sat bolt upright.

'That's a terrible thing to say! There must be
someone.'

'My father died when I was very young, my mother's
remarried three times since then and at the moment
she's living in California with a man who's five years
younger than I am,' came his stark reply. 'I've three
stepfathers and countless stepbrothers and sisters, but I
never see any of them. My mother's marriages lasted
such a short time that we hardly even had time to get to
know each other before she'd moved on to the next
husband and another batch of instant relatives.'

A small ache of pity started up inside her.

'You must have been awfully lonely,' she said in a low voice.

He merely shrugged.

'I learnt to cope with it.'

Sophie remembered her first impression of him: a lone wolf. That judgement had been even more accurate than she'd realised at the time.

Another question hovered on her lips, but he cut in and forestalled it, as if he was tired of talking about himself.

'What about you, Lady Sophia Carlton? I've called you spoilt and pampered often enough—but was I right?'

'Certainly not!' she retorted spiritedly. Then honesty forced her to give a rueful smile. 'Well, perhaps partly right,' she conceded, flicking back a strand of black hair. 'I'm an only child, and I didn't turn up until my parents were well into their forties and resigned to not having any children. They were slightly disappointed when I turned out to be a girl, not a son and heir, but that lasted for only about ten seconds. Then they fell over backwards with delight at having produced something so incredibly perfect—their words, not mine!' she added hastily, seeing Jareth's dark brows beginning to rise expressively.

'And ever since then, I suppose you've had just about everything you've ever wanted,' he remarked caustically.

Sophie gave a small grimace.

'I'm afraid so,' she answered in an apologetic tone. 'Finishing school, all the clothes I ever needed, a generous allowance—I've had the lot.'

'So why did you run away?' he asked perceptively.

She glared at him indignantly.

'You're the one who's running away, not me! I'm

going to join David, to be married. That's not running
away!'

The blue eyes were studying her so intently that they
seemed to be probing right inside her soul. In the end,
she turned her head away, trying slightly desperately to
escape from that piercing gaze.

'You haven't told your parents—or anyone—about
this forthcoming marriage of yours,' Jareth went on
thoughtfully. 'Why all the secrecy, Sophie? You're not
ashamed of David, are you?'

At that, she gasped out loud.

'*Ashamed* of him! Of course not, he's the kindest,
most decent man I've ever met, and you've absolutely
no right to insinuate that he isn't!'

'I've never implied anything of the kind,' he
remarked calmly. 'I may have said once or twice that he
struck me as a little dull, but since I've never met the
man, I could well be wrong about that. Or perhaps you
want a quiet, uneventful life, no great highs or lows, just
a gentle plod towards middle age?'

'You're hateful!' she snapped.

He remained infuriatingly cool.

'Why are you getting so worked up? Or have I
painted a picture of the future that's too accurate for
your liking?' He paused, regarding her thoughtfully
before adding in a reflective tone, 'You're not a retiring
little mouse, Sophie, far from it. My guess is that you're
running off to marry David because life at home got just
too suffocating for you. Doting parents who love you
just a little too much, not giving you room to breathe, to
live your own life. In the end you broke loose, simply
had to find some way to escape. This whirlwind
romance with David gave you the perfect opportunity,
so you grabbed it with both hands.'

She glared at him. That was typical of him, crediting

her with a rotten motive like that! All right, she conceded to herself with some reluctance, she *had* wanted to get away from home, try and stand on her own two feet, do something useful with her life. She hadn't needed to come halfway across the world to do that, though. There were plenty of charitable organisations back home crying out for willing helpers. No, she was here because David's idealism had lit a responding spark inside her, given her the impetus she'd needed to throw off her old life and carve out a new, purposeful future for herself. And how dared he insinuate that she had any other motive!

'You make it sound as if I'm just using David,' she accused resentfully.

'Well, aren't you?' came Jareth's almost clinically detached query.

'Of course not!' Sophie tossed back at him furiously, and was horrified to find that her voice sounded as if she were trying to convince herself, not him. 'I love David,' she announced firmly, a hint of stubborn determination creeping into her voice, 'I *do* love him.'

The blue eyes flickered perceptibly, but his face remained curiously immobile, almost as if he were deliberately keeping his features totally expressionless.

'And does he love you? Love you the way that you were meant to be loved?'

Sophie struggled hard to remain as calm as he was.

'What on earth do you mean?'

Still no outward emotion showed on his face; she was rather unnerved by this unnatural display of self-control.

'No two women are alike,' he said after a slight pause. 'Some are cool inside, some warm, some burning hot. Unless you can find the right partner to match your own special temperature, life can be pretty miserable.'

'I presume we're talking about sex now,' she commented disdainfully. 'Well, I happen to believe that sex isn't the beginning and the end of everything, there are a lot of things far more important.'

'So there are,' agreed Jareth, to her surprise. 'But if the sex isn't right, it's surprising how many other things tend to go wrong. Have you slept with David?'

His casual question sent a bright flare of colour into her face.

'That's none of your damned business!'

'Obviously you haven't,' he remarked with infuriating insight. 'Then take care, Sophie. You're a girl who needs a lot of loving. Make sure you find a man who can give it to you.'

Her temper finally flared out of all control.

'Then that rules you out, doesn't it?' she flung back at him cruelly. 'After all, you've already admitted you've been impotent ever since that plane crash!'

The instant the words were out of her mouth, she wanted to die of shame. That had been a horrible, horrible thing to say, the kind of bitchy response she always despised in other women.

'I'm sorry,'she mumbled under her breath. 'Oh God, I'm sorry, I didn't mean to say that.'

She heard him draw in a sharp breath, then another.

'Go to bed, Sophie,' he ordered at last in a taut voice.

'You made me so mad,' she said miserably. 'I just wanted to hit back at you. Please, Jareth, can't you understand——?'

'Go to bed!'

He had never used that tone of voice to her before, and it frightened her half to death. Grabbing her blanket, she fled to a dark corner, where she lay huddled on the ground with her back to him so that she wouldn't have to see his face, then burying her own face in the blanket so he wouldn't hear her hot, muffled tears of remorse.

CHAPTER SIX

IN the morning they ate breakfast and prepared to leave in an atmosphere of unnatural politeness. They were like two strangers who had just met and who were carefully observing all the formal courtesies.

For a long time they travelled without speaking at all. Then towards the end of the morning, Jareth edged his camel alongside Sophie's. She shot him a furtive glance from under her long lashes as the two animals plodded along side by side and saw, to her utter relief, that those brooding shadows no longer darkened his face, his eyes were a clear, bright blue and free of that dangerous glitter which always lit them when his temper was slowly simmering.

'What do you plan to do when you finally reach Hajjar?' he asked casually after a few minutes of unexpectedly companionable silence.

She stiffened slightly.

'You know what I'm going to do. I'm going to marry David.'

His shoulders lifted in a brief, impatient shrug.

'Yes, I know that, you've already made it tiresomely clear. What I mean is, how are you going to occupy yourself? Presumably David will be working most of the day, so what will you do while he's away? Your Arabic's pretty poor, so you won't be able to chat to the other women. Not that you'd have much in common with them, anyway,' he added reflectively.

Sophie gritted her teeth. Why was he so obsessed with her relationship with David and the kind of life she was going to lead with him? She was getting thoroughly fed up with these endless questions. As she was on the point of telling him that it was none of his business, a sudden dart of guilt shot through her as she remembered last night, how her runaway tongue had catapulted her straight into that awful situation. With an effort she curbed her irritation and answered him civilly.

'I'm going to learn Arabic properly, of course. And as soon as I can speak it fairly fluently, I'm going to try and help David in his work.'

To her annoyance, Jareth seemed distinctly unimpressed.

'Do you have any experience? Any qualifications?'

'Well—no——' she floundered slightly.

'How about medical training? Even a first-aid certificate? Then you could help with basic health and hygiene problems.'

Damn him! Sophie thought furiously. He knew perfectly well that she'd led a shamefully useless life up until now. But that was why she was here, because she'd grown tired of being a butterfly, someone who was gorgeous to look at but had no real role in life, no chance to use the brains which she knew she possessed.

'If you've no qualifications of any kind,' went on Jareth relentlessly, 'what possible use will you be to David?'

Her volatile temper crashed out of control again.

'If I can't do anything else, at least I'll be able to keep him warm in bed at night!' she hissed.

And that put a halt to any more conversation for the rest of the day. Jareth kicked his camel so hard that it moved far ahead of hers, and from then on she had a perfect view of his rigid back as he stayed several yards in front of her.

To her relief there was no sign of Sheik Rashid or any

of his men. By mid-afternoon Sophie was stiff and aching from the unflagging pace Jareth set, and not looking forward to another night sleeping on the hard, cold ground. Then she saw a small town in the distance, and sighed thankfully as Jareth changed direction and began to head towards it.

It was nearly an hour later before they were finally plodding down a main street that was lined with mud-brick houses and shops and, further on, some yellow government buildings, their faded splendour a relic from the colonial days.

Jareth reined his camel to a halt in front of the largest of the buildings.

'We need somewhere to stay for the night. The simplest thing would probably be to ask here, at the police station. They'll almost certainly know someone who would be willing to put us up.'

Her head filled with tantalising visions of a hot meal and a soft bed, Sophie slid down from her camel and stretched her aching limbs.

'Better get your papers ready before we go in,' warned Jareth, digging his own passport, visa and travel permits out from an inner pocket in his shirt. 'You know what the red tape's like around here. No one goes anywhere unless all their papers are in order.'

With a tired sigh, Sophie began to burrow around inside one of the saddlebags. A couple of minutes later she was still scrabbling through her possessions, only more frantically now.

'Hurry up,' urged Jareth a trifle impatiently.

Sophie raised her head slowly and a little fearfully.

'I can't find them,' she mumbled, a clear tremor in her voice. 'Jareth, they've *gone*!'

'Oh hell,' he said heavily. 'Are you sure?'

'Absolutely positive,' she sniffed unhappily, rubbing

her eyes with the back of her hand. 'I've been through everything several times. I had all the papers in a small leather wallet, and it just isn't there. It must have fallen out. Jareth, what am I going to do?'

He looked down at her forlorn face, wiped away a stray tear from her cheek with one finger, then gave a brief sigh.

'Who would ever believe one small girl could cause so many problems?' he remarked with resignation. 'All right, Sophie,' he went on hastily, 'don't start to cry again. I'll try and sort this out.'

She blinked her damp lashes hopefully.

'Can you think of a way round this?'

'I'd better,' he answered rather grimly, 'or we're both going to be in a lot of trouble. For a start, let's get away from the police station before some official comes out and starts asking a lot of awkward questions.'

He led her quickly down a narrow side street, and a few minutes later they found themselves standing in a tiny, deserted square.

'All right,' said Jareth without preamble, 'let's go through your things one more time, just to make sure the papers haven't got tucked away in a corner.'

'They're not there,' Sophie insisted miserably. 'I've lost them.'

All the same, he went through every inch of her luggage, his face growing more and more grim as he failed to find anything.

Tossing the last bag to one side, he released a frustrated sigh.

'Okay, you're right. They're not there.'

'Can't I get duplicates?' she questioned in a small voice.

His blue eyes flickered with impatience.

'This isn't some nice safe European country,' he

reminded her tersely. 'There isn't a British Embassy just around the corner, full of staff all falling over themselves to get you a set of fresh papers. This is an isolated little town in the back of beyond, and the local police have complete authority here. Once they find out your papers are missing——'

'Can't we just scoot out of here before anyone asks to see my papers?' she said, beginning to feel slightly dizzy now with apprehension.

Jareth's face darkened.

'It would only be a matter of time before they caught up with us,' he answered shortly. 'A couple of Europeans riding around on camels isn't exactly an everyday sight around here, chances are some official's already noticed our arrival. We might manage to slip out of this town before being questioned, but they'll only be waiting for us in the next town, or the one after that. We can't keep running for ever, they'll catch up with us in the end.'

Sophie chewed her lip nervously.

'Perhaps they won't bother to check on us,' she suggested, although not too hopefully. 'Why should they go to so much trouble over just a couple of people passing through?'

'Come on, Sophie,' said Jareth roughly, 'you know better than that. You've been in this country long enough to know how things work. If you're a foreigner, you don't go anywhere without the proper documents and travel permits. I've seen what happens to people who're picked up without the proper papers, and believe me, I wouldn't want to see it happen to you.'

Despite the heat, her teeth began to chatter.

'What's—what's the worst that could happen?' she asked, staring at him with huge, fearful eyes.

'You really want to know?'

She nodded shakily.

'Deportation,' he told her bluntly. 'And don't say they wouldn't go that far,' he warned her as he saw the disbelief in her eyes. 'They certainly would.'

The thought of being thrown out of the country when she'd gone through so much, and was so close to finally being reunited with David, filled her with total dismay.

'Surely there's some way we can get round it——?' she began, then stopped abruptly as she saw the bright flare of his eyes.

'For God's sake, Sophie!' he exploded, rounding on her and giving her a brief shake, 'don't you understand even now just how much trouble you're in?.'

She glared back at him.

'Of course I understand,' she shot back. 'You've made it perfectly clear. There's every chance I'm going to be deported.'

He growled irritably under his breath.

'And how exactly do you suppose they'll go about it?' he demanded.

A little warily, she met his blazing gaze full on, wilting slightly under its intensity.

'What do you mean?' she asked in a voice that was suddenly tremulous.

He let go of her, took a few restless steps away from her, then prowled back again.

'Do you think they're going to buy you a first-class ticket on the first available plane back home?' he challenged. 'Take you to the airport in a taxi, carry your bags on to the plane?'

'Well, I suppose not,' she conceded a little reluctantly.

'You suppose not?' he repeated with heavy sarcasm. His hands gripped her arms again, his fingers sinking deeply into her delicate skin until she seemed to feel the blood pulsing through his fingertips. 'I'll tell you exactly what they'll do, because I've seen it happen to others who got themselves into the same predicament. Firstly, they'll sling you into jail. Then they'll keep you there for a very long time while they fill in reams and reams of forms, because bureaucracy rules here and no one does anything without completing a stack of paperwork. Only when every one of those questions on every one of those forms is filled in to their satisfaction—and who knows how long that'll take?——' he added grimly, 'will they even *consider* letting you leave.'

Sophie swallowed hard, feeling distinctly sick.

'They'll really put me in jail?' she said in a voice that quavered horribly.

'There's every chance they'll do precisely that,' he assured her grimly.

She shuddered.

'I couldn't stand that, I know I couldn't.'

'No, I don't think you could,' Jareth agreed tautly. 'I've seen the jails in this country, and believe me, I wouldn't want my worst enemy to spend too much time in one of them.'

'Isn't there anything we can do?' she begged miserably. 'Jareth, there must be *something*! I'd do anything to get out of going to jail, absolutely anything!'

He was silent for such a very long time that she thought he wasn't going to answer her. When she finally found the courage to raise her head and look at him, she discovered he was standing very still, staring over to the far side of the square.

She followed his gaze and found he was looking at a small, square building attached to a rather ramshackle house. Not knowing why he was finding it of such interest, she stared closer, then finally noticed the lopsided cross over the door, and realised that it was a small church. Perhaps he was going to go and pray for some divine guidance, she thought rather irreverently. She scuffled her feet restlessly in the dust, wishing he would say something. This long silence was setting all her nerves on edge.

She risked a quick sideways glance at his face and saw that his features were drawn into a dark frown, as if he were thinking of something that he didn't find particularly to his liking. Then he abruptly lifted his head, as if he had suddenly reached a decision.

'Would you really do anything to avoid going to jail?' he asked tersely.

Sophie nodded eagerly.

'Yes, I would, I promise I would.'

He seemed to hesitate for a couple more seconds, then he swung round to face her.

'Would you marry me?' he challenged her, to her total amazement.

For a moment she was rather cross with him.

'This is hardly the time for jokes!' she snapped back edgily.

'No joke,' he assured her, in a voice that was devoid of all emotion. 'It's probably the only way you're going to get out of this mess, Sophie. You have to marry me.'

She stared at him in utter disbelief.

'I don't believe you. You're making it up.'

He shrugged.

'Suit yourself. If you can think of another solution, that's fine by me. I'm not exactly eager to march up the aisle with you.'

Her mind seemed to have gone a complete blank, she just couldn't think straight. What he was proposing was absolutely preposterous, she'd never agree to go through with such a mad scheme, never!

Not even to stay out of jail? whispered a treacherous little voice inside her head.

Sophie groaned out loud in confusion and despair.

'I don't understand any of this,' she muttered slightly desperately. '*Why* do I have to marry you? What difference would it make?'

'It's possible it won't make any difference at all,' Jareth admitted. 'But on the other hand, there's a good chance it'll swing things in our favour. Remember, Women's Lib is completely unknown in this country,' he reminded her. 'Out here, a wife is regarded as her husband's possession. Once we're married, in the eyes of the law you'll belong to me, I'll be regarded as being totally responsible for you. With luck, it won't matter that you don't have any papers, because as my wife you won't have any status.'

Her eyes glowed indignantly.

'That's barbaric!' she protested furiously. 'That puts me on about the same par as a—well, a camel or a goat, just something that belongs to you!'

'That's right,' he agreed, with a faintly mocking grin. Then the grin swiftly vanished and his mouth settled into a much more serious line. 'I don't even know if we *can* get married without producing the right papers,' he warned her, 'but if we can manage it, there's a good chance it'll keep you out of jail. I'm willing to go through with it if you are.'

'But I don't *want* to marry you!' she wailed in dismay. 'I want to marry David.'

'I'm not exactly thrilled by the prospect either,' he assured her with some feeling, 'but I can't see any other way out of this mess. Believe me, if there were, I'd take it.'

A curious weakness started up in the pit of her stomach as she realised that she couldn't think of any other solution either.

'What——' She gulped, tried again. 'What'll happen after the wedding?'

'With luck, we'll be free to move on without any problems with the police.'

She shook her head nervously.

'No, I mean what'll happen to us?'

The blue eyes suddenly became very cool.

'I've no intention of holding you to your marriage vows, if that's what's worrying you. Eventually, we'll get an annulment. It shouldn't be too difficult to arrange, once we explain the circumstances.'

'And then I'll be free to marry David?'

'You'll be free to marry anyone you damned well please!' Jareth growled back in an unexpected explosion of bad temper.

Thinking that he was irritated by the prospect of having to marry her in the first place, Sophie stared at him anxiously as he gathered up the reins of the camels, then began to lead them across the square.

'Where are we going?' she asked nervously as she hurried to catch up with him.

He nodded in front of him.

'To the church. There's obviously a small Christian community here, so let's try and find whoever's in charge and see if there's any chance of this marriage taking place.'

He seemed to be assuming that she was just going to meekly fall in with his outrageous plan! On the verge of protesting vigorously, she suddenly shut up as it dawned on her that the consequences of defying him would probably be horribly unpleasant. She'd never seen the inside of a jail in this country, but she was absolutely sure they were every bit as unpleasant as Jareth had promised, and the thought of being slung into one indefinitely made her blood run cold. And it wasn't as if

this marriage was going to be for real. At least, it would
be real enough to fool the authorities, but it would be
strictly temporary, she reminded herself, and there
would certainly be no problem about getting an
annulment on the grounds of non-consummation. A
faint flush covered her skin as those last thoughts
chased their way through her head, then they were at
the door of the small church and Jareth was tethering
the camels, then pushing the door open and walking
inside.

Her first impression was of dust and disrepair. The
windows were grimy, the few rows of chairs so
ramshackle that it was a miracle they were still
standing. Then a door at the far end opened and a short,
dumpy little man rolled in.

Sophie stared at his bright red face and slightly glazed
eyes, then tugged on Jareth's sleeve.

'Is that the priest?' she whispered.

'It rather looks like it,' he answered drily.

'Is he sober?' she asked in horrified fascination.

Before Jareth had a chance to reply, the man wove his
way towards them.

'I'm Father Donoghue,' he announced, his face
breaking into a huge smile. 'Welcome to my small
church. My congregation is—well, fairly small nowa-
days,' he admitted, with a rueful shrug, 'so I'm always
pleased to see two newcomers.'

'I'm afraid we're only passing through, Father,'
Jareth said smoothly. 'But when we saw your church,
we came straight over. You see, we want to get married.'

The priest looked surprised, then he nodded his head
vigorously.

'It'll be a pleasure, I can't remember when we last had
a wedding in this church. Of course,' he went on

doubtfully, 'there'll be certain formalities to go through first——'

'We're in rather a hurry,' interrupted Jareth persuasively, taking hold of the priest's arm and gently leading him to one side. 'I couldn't help noticing your church is badly in need of repair. I wonder if perhaps a small donation would be of some help?'

At the sight of Jareth's wallet, Father Donoghue's eyes fairly shone. The two men's voices were lowered so that Sophie could no longer hear what they were saying, then she saw a tactful exchange of what looked like a substantial amount of money. As Father Donoghue tucked it away beneath the voluminous folds of his robe, Jareth swiftly walked back to Sophie.

'Okay,' he said in a low tone, 'he's agreed to go through with the ceremony straightaway. Look pleased, kiss me, as if you're absolutely thrilled at the thought of getting married. I don't want Father Donoghue to think that we're anything more than a couple of lovers who just can't wait to make it legal!'

Suddenly hopelessly shy, she hung back uncertainly, lowering her lashes so that she wouldn't have to actually look at him.

'Oh, for heaven's sake——' he muttered under his breath, then he reached out and roughly pulled her close to him, so that they were touching from head to toe. An instant later, his mouth closed over hers, and it was just like the last time he'd kissed her, an explosion of reaction right through her body, as if someone had set off a string of fire-crackers in all her nerve-ends.

Terrified of her own body and the erratic way it was behaving, Sophie instinctively pressed her hands against his chest, as if to push him away; then her eyes shot open wide in wonder as she felt the hard, rhythmic beat of his heart against her palms. It was almost like

touching his soul, a dazzlingly intimate sensation which
sent flutters of wonder right through her. His lips moved
again on hers, filling her with wave after wave of
sweetness, and she thought for a brief instant that she
felt a quick stirring inside him, a swift flare of
answering response.

Then it was over, he was smoothly moving away from
her, and she wanted to cry out in disappointment and
frustration. Her blurred gaze rested on Father Donoghue's
face, she saw him smiling at her indulgently, and
she had to turn away so that neither of them could see
the awful confusion that had suddenly started to eat
away inside of her.

Father Donoghue took a couple of steps forward.

'I realise that this marriage was a spur-of-the-moment
decision,' he said, lowering his tone tactfully, 'so might I
ask if you have a ring?'

Sophie glanced at Jareth in dismay. It was something
they hadn't even thought of.

Father Donoghue intercepted her glance, gave them
an encouraging smile.

'Don't worry,' he assured them cheerfully, 'if you
don't mind waiting here for just a short while, I'm sure
I'll be able to find something suitable. No need to thank
me,' he called back at them as he trotted off, 'and you
can pay me for it afterwards. Cash would be preferable,
of course, but I'll take a traveller's cheque if that's all
you've got!'

As he hurried out of the door at the back of the
church, Sophie turned to Jareth indignantly.

'He's just a con man!'

'As long as he's authorised to marry us, I don't care if
he's Father Christmas,' responded Jareth tersely.
'Remember the alternative, Sophie. A long stretch in
jail, then deportation.'

'I'm being blackmailed into this marriage!' she flung at him accusingly, her temper as frayed now as her nerves.

Jareth shook his head.

'You're free to back out any time you want. Just say the word and we'll call the whole thing off.'

If only she could! But the awful prospect of jail was more than she could face. And she clung on to the thought that this marriage was only temporary, in a few weeks it would be annulled and it would be as if the whole thing had never happened.

Nevertheless, she was actually shaking by the time Father Donoghue returned, clutching a thin gold ring in his hand.

'This should do nicely,' he said cheerfully. 'Now, shall we get this marriage ceremony under way?'

It seemed to be over almost before it had begun, and afterwards Sophie could remember hardly any of it. The gold band was on her finger, though—a perfect fit—and Father Donoghue's red face was beaming with pleasure.

'If you'll just wait here for a few minutes, I'll make out your marriage certificate,' he told them.

Marriage certificate. The words echoed round and round inside Sophie's head. So she'd actually done it! She'd married Jareth Kingsley. Nervously, she shot a furtive glance at her husband, relaxed slightly as she saw his dark, familiar features. Then he turned to meet her gaze and gave her an unexpectedly warm smile, his eyes a strangely vivid shade of blue.

And quite suddenly, it didn't seem at all strange to be Sophia Kingsley instead of Sophia Carlton. And that was probably the most unnerving discovery she'd made since embarking on this insane charade.

CHAPTER SEVEN

BY the time the marriage certificate had been made out and they'd signed it, the light was beginnning to fade fast outside the window. Father Donoghue glanced at them thoughtfully.

'It's too late for you to travel any further today. Do you have somewhere to stay tonight?'

Jareth shook his head.

'No, we don't.'

'I've a spare room that you're welcome to use,' the priest told them. 'Would you care to be my guests for the night?'

'That's very kind of you,' answered Jareth. 'My wife and I would be delighted to accept your offer.'

Completely shaken by that casual reference to her new marital status, Sophie stumbled after him as they collected their belongings, then followed the priest round to the house that adjoined the church.

'The spare bedroom is upstairs,' Father Donoghue told them, then he winked wickedly. 'I expect you want to go up right away!'

To her fury, Sophie found herself blushing furiously.

'There, there,' he said kindly, 'no need for shyness or embarrassment. I might be a man of God, but I understand the ways of the world well enough. Now, up you go, and you can be sure no one will disturb you until the morning.'

Sophie slunk up the stairs, then let out a small groan of dismay as she went into the bedroom. The main feature of the sparsely furnished room was a huge double bed. Apart from that, there was only a chest of drawers, a wardrobe and a rickety wooden chair.

Jareth followed her in, then closed the door behind him. She saw his gaze travel round the room, then a spark of amusement flickered deep in his eyes.

'That bed's large enough to accommodate even the most passionate of newlywed couples,' he commented.

Already on edge as she was, his remark seemed to touch a particularly raw nerve.

'That's a disgusting thing to say!' she accused stiffly.

His gaze slewed round to fix on her steadily until she felt the heat beginning to bubble up under her skin, and she would have given almost anything to be a hundred, thousand miles away from here.

'Why pretend to be so prudish, so easily shocked? Unless you learn to accept the kind of woman you are, you're going to have a very miserable married life,' Jareth told her softly at last. 'You might be all cool sophistication on the surface, but underneath you're burning hot. Don't bother to deny it,' he added as he saw the anger begin to show on her face. 'I might have lived like a monk these past few months, but before that I was far from celibate. Believe me, I know about these things.'

She believed him! In fact, it was probably that deep-buried streak of sexual experience and worldliness that still scared her about him. Ruthlessly suppressed though it was, lying as dormant as a hibernating animal ever since the accident, it still simmered below the surface, like a sleeping tiger. Something inside her recognised it, responded to it, secretly fantasised over what would happen if the tiger ever awoke——

Gasping slightly, she shook her head in a vain effort to clear it of the weird thoughts that whirled round inside it.

'Since I'm not going to spend my married life with you,' she flung back fiercely in self-defence, 'I don't see that my prudishness is any concern of yours!'

For a moment she thought he was going to furiously contradict her, she saw the storm clouds darkening his eyes. Then they rolled away again, the gentian-blue eyes became clear and deliberately blank.

'You're right, of course,' he said politely. 'It's none of my business at all.' He took out his wallet and flicked through the traveller's cheques inside. 'I'm going down to pay Father Donoghue for that ring you're wearing. Since you're determined to be so modest tonight, you might like to get undressed while I'm out of the room.'

'Let me pay half towards the ring,' Sophie offered.

'No!'

The terseness of his tone made her jump. Before she had time to argue with him, he had swung round and swiftly left the room, banging the door rather noisily behind him.

She wasted a couple of minutes just standing there, fuming. He was so bad-tempered, arrogant, pigheaded—and he was beginning to know her and understand her far too well for comfort! Then she realised she was wasting precious time, he'd be back soon and she'd have lost her chance to get undressed in private.

Rummaging through her bundle of clothes, she dug out a pair of thick warm winceyette pyjamas. In the desert, she had usually slept in her clothes, but tonight she would have a chance to wear her night things for a change.

Holding them up, she wrinkled her nose as she studied them. Not exactly the most glamorous nightwear in the world. Her gaze slid across to the small package which held those last-minute items she'd rushed out to buy before leaving London. Then her fingers guiltily crept over, opened the package, took out one of the garments inside.

It had been wickedly expensive, yet worth every penny. Even crumpled as it was after its long journey, when she shook out the white satin folds, it still took her breath away. It was the most gorgeous thing she'd ever owned, the kind of nightdress that every girl should wear at least once in her life.

The winceyette pyjamas were tossed aside as an idea took root inside her head. Holding her breath, she slid the soft wisp of satin over her head, felt the shining folds clinging to the supple curves of her body, provocatively covering and yet allowing the merest glimmer of skin to show beneath the glistening material. Then she brushed her hair vigorously until it positively shone, the black strands contrasting startlingly with the white satin.

'Right,' she muttered, putting down the brush and standing with her hands on her hips. 'I've had just about enough of Mr Jareth Kingsley's personal remarks. Let's see *him* sweat for a change, see how cool he manages to stay once he's got an eyeful of this!'

She walked over to the bed, then stretched out on it in a deliberately sensual pose. The evening light was just beginning to fade, lending a mysterious sheen to her satin-clad body, and she hoped Jareth wouldn't be too long. It would be completely dark soon, then the whole effect would be totally wasted.

Her pulses started to thump away at a strangely fast speed as she finally heard his footsteps outside the door. As he came into the room, she threw a deliberately languorous look at him, then stretched her lithe limbs provocatively.

She thought he checked for just the briefest of moments. Then he kicked off his shoes, stripped off his shirt, and stood there in just the loose cotton trousers which fitted so snugly around his lean waist.

'Haven't you got anything warmer to wear?' he queried casually. 'You'll be chilly later tonight, once it starts to get cold.'

The man was made of ice! she decided furiously. There was just no way to get to him.

Turning sulkily on to her side, she pulled the rather threadbare quilt up to her chin and glared at him.

'I suppose you're not going to do the decent thing and let me have this bed to myself?' she challenged huffily.

'I'm certainly not going to spend the night in the chair,' he agreed. 'Why all the hassle? This won't be the first time we've slept together.'

'That doesn't make it right!' Sophie muttered in a furious undertone.

'What's the matter?' he probed silkily. 'Still nervous that I might tell David about all the nights we've spent together?'

'David's a decent, understanding man,' she shot back at him instantly. 'I'm not scared of him hearing the truth.'

'Poor Sophie,' murmured Jareth with gentle mockery, 'having to spend the rest of your life with a decent, understanding man. What will you do for excitement after I've gone, my lady?'

It shook her more than she cared to admit to hear him call her by that affectionately teasing name again. Dragging the quilt tighter around her, she moved to the very far edge of the bed.

'I'm tired,' she told him stiltedly. 'I want to sleep. Would you kindly stop talking?'

She felt the bed dip under his weight as he slid in beside her, then heard the light, steady sound of his breathing as he seemed to drift quickly into a deep sleep. Soothed by the rhythmic sound, she found her own eyelids slowly closing; soon she, too, was drifting away into the velvety darkness.

When she woke up again, she had no idea what time it was. It was still very dark, though, the only light coming from a pale beam of moonlight drifting in through the window. And the temperature had plummeted, as it always did during the hours of darkness, she could feel the cool air against her slightly flushed skin.

Yet she wasn't cold despite the flimsiness of her nightdress and the thinness of the quilt which covered her. An instant later, a tiny quiver ran through her as she realised why.

They'd both moved during their sleep, abandoning the outer edges of the bed and moving towards the centre. Now they were lying in a warm, comfortable tangle of arms and legs, sharing their body heat, their skin touching in so many places that she felt as if they were welded together.

Pulses thundering, she knew perfectly well she ought to roll away. A couple of times she actually tried to, but her body seemed to have gone on strike, her limbs absolutely refused to co-operate. Not a single muscle would obey her, they felt stupidly, uselessly weak and helpless. Even her bones seemed to have melted, she was like a puddle of jelly. She'd never felt like this in her life before, and it absolutely terrified her.

She had no idea how long she lay there like that, trying to make some sense of what was happening to her, keeping her eyes resolutely shut and hoping frantically that she'd just fall asleep again, plunge into the relief of oblivion.

Then Jareth's hand, which had been resting on her stomach, moved a fraction of an inch, and her entire body jerked in instant reaction.

'How much longer are you going to pretend to be

asleep?' he murmured in her ear. 'You've been awake for at least half an hour.'

Sophie swallowed hard.

'And how long have *you* been awake?' she asked in a quavery voice.

'Ever since we went to bed,' came his slightly husky admission. 'Did you really expect me to sleep after that sexy little display you put on?'

'I was mad at you, that was all,' she said, her tone still horribly unsteady. 'I just wanted to get my own back for once.'

'Well, you've managed that all right,' he assured her drily. 'I can't remember when I last spent a more restless night. Of course,' he went on with a touch of self-mockery, 'when I share my bed with a beautiful girl, I don't usually sleep very much anyway.'

'But that was before your accident,' she reminded him with fast-growing nervousness. 'I mean, since then you've not wanted to share your bed with anyone. That's why it's all right for us to sleep together like this, because you don't want to——'

Her voice trailed away completely as one of his fingers traced a rhythmic pattern on her upper arm.

'Because I don't want to what?' he prompted gently.

Oh lord, this was getting out of control! She could feel the situation running away from her, and she didn't know what on earth to do about it.

'You know perfectly well what I mean,' she snapped, fear lending a sharp edge to her voice.

'Oh yes,' he mused reflectively. 'Because I don't want to do this?' His fingers slid from her arm, wandered up to the base of her throat where they lingered provocatively against her silky skin. 'Or this?' he purred relentlessly, and before she could protest, his hand had drifted to the spot where the soft swell of her breast began. And there his hand stopped, playing gently around the edges, setting off those tiny fire-crackers with which she was becoming achingly familiar.

A faint groan escaped her, she just couldn't stop it, and she knew he'd heard it because his hand instantly became still, he almost seemed to stop breathing.

And at that instant, something between them irrevocably changed, she sensed it so clearly that it might almost have been a physical shifting of the forces that pulsed around them. The night became very still, very silent, the beam of moonlight crept over the bed, covered them with a silver light so that their bodies seemed almost to glow. Raising himself up on to one arm, Jareth threw back the quilt, then stared down at her, his eyes shining luminously in the pale light.

'Ever since we met, you've been playing games with me, my lady,' he told her in a hoarse tone. 'Teasing me, provoking me, slowly driving me mad. Well, tonight we're going to play a very different game. And since it's one where I know all the rules and you don't, you'd better pay very close attention as we go along and do exactly as I say.'

Sophie stared up at him with wide-eyed apprehension.

'And if I don't?' she murmured shakily.

'Then you'll have to pay a forfeit.'

She was dreaming, she had to be dreaming! Yet she had an awful feeling that she wasn't, that this was all nerve-achingly real.

'W—what kind of f—forfeit?' she somehow managed to get out through chattering teeth.

He seemed to consider her question for a moment.

'I'll decide as we go along,' he told her softly at last. 'For instance, it might be something like this——'

One knowing fingertip lightly touched the hard peak

of her nipple where it thrust against the soft satin of her nightdress. The fire-cracker became an exploding fountain, the cascade of sparks shot through her body, lighting a hundred, a thousand other tiny fires.

'Like it?' Jareth questioned almost lazily. 'But it would be so much nicer if the nightdress was out of the way completely. If you're a very good girl, I'll show you just *how* nice it can be.'

Sophie's eyes shone with amazement. How could it possibly be nicer? But this was all a dream anyway, it had to be a dream, if she were awake she would never be behaving like this, just lying here, letting this man—her husband! she realised with a tiny sense of shock—do exactly what he liked to her.

And if it *was* a dream, then it was all right, it didn't really matter what happened. She certainly felt as if she were floating through some delicious fantasy, her body was so light, it almost felt that it might drift away if she let it.

She languidly raised one arm, half expecting to see it float right up into the air, as if it didn't even belong to her. Instead, though, her fingers brushed against warm, supple skin, and she felt the light grazing of crisp hair, the outline of a powerful rib cage.

Jareth caught her fingers, then a little roughly pushed them away.

'Don't touch me,' he warned. 'Not unless you want things to move a great deal faster than I planned. Self-control isn't exactly my strong point at the moment, not after all these months.'

Obediently, Sophie let her hand fall back on to the pillow.

'Good girl,' he approved softly. 'That deserves a reward. What would you like? A kiss, perhaps?'

With shameful eagerness, she waited for the brush of

his lips against hers, remembering those other kisses he'd given her, with such delicious results.

Instead, though, his mouth slowly explored the side of her neck, wandered down to her throat, left in its wake a scalding trail that actually seemed to burn.

'Did you like that, too?' he asked huskily. 'There are so many things you're going to like. Although I'm not sure we're going to manage to get through every single one of them tonight,' he added with a breathless laugh. His gaze drifted downwards. 'That's a very sexy nightdress,' he went on, his fingers stroking the soft material in a deeply sensual rhythm. 'When I first saw you wearing it, something seemed to explode inside my head. I nearly threw you on to the bed and made love to you right then and there.'

'I didn't think you'd even noticed it,' she whispered.

'I noticed it,' he assured her thickly. 'But now it's going to have to come off. It's gorgeous, but your skin is even more gorgeous and I want to feel every inch of it.'

To her bewilderment, her body was already raising itself so that he could slip the thin straps from her shoulders. Didn't she have a will of her own any more? Was she totally helpless, caught in the strands of the sensual web this man was weaving around her, completely hypnotised by the subtle combination of his deadly skilful hands and velvet voice?

Then the nightdress was gently drawn down to her waist, she caught her breath as she saw his face as he stared at the perfection of her breasts.

'You're very beautiful, my lady,' he said in a voice that had suddenly lost all its steadiness. 'Very beautiful, very bright, very brave. And I want you so much that I'm nearly going out of my mind.'

Yet there was still a vestige of self-control and patience left in his hands as he lovingly traced the curved silhouette of her quivering body. Then he moved a little closer, leant over her so that the light covering of hair on his chest rasped against the very tips of her breasts, keeping the same distance all the time so that the only point of contact between them was at those twin ultra-sensitive spots. Wave after wave of longing broke over her, the world shrank to the few square feet of space which their two bodies occupied. Before she could stop them, her hands had crept round Jareth's waist, begun to explore the powerful muscles, which instantly tensed under her touch, standing out in sharp relief under the hot, supple skin.

He drew in a swift, ragged breath, then another.

'You're breaking the rules,' he muttered in a shaken voice. 'Didn't I warn you that wasn't allowed? I claim another forfeit from your ladyship.'

Dizzily, Sophie waited in tormented anticipation, feeling feverishly overheated, as if she might catch fire completely if this went on for very much longer.

He kept her waiting for several more agonisingly long seconds—all part of the forfeit, she realised hazily. Then his touch, when it did finally come, was at first so soft, so subtle, that she scarcely felt it, it was like a feather whispering against her skin, playing lightly, almost teasingly with the soft swell of her breast, sliding up and down the full curve like a child with a new toy. Yet the sensations which that featherlight touch sent crashing through her were anything but childish, her skin seemed to glow, her body moved restlessly, instinctively seeking closer contact.

'Keep still,' Jareth ordered softly, and although it was torture, she didn't dare disobey, somehow managing to lie quite motionless as that pattern of exotic caresses played over her flushed skin, setting up an unfamiliar, throbbing ache deep inside her. Up and down, up and down moved those tormenting fingers, trailing fire in their wake, inflicting their sensual torture. Then when she knew she couldn't stand it one instant longer, she would have to move her rigid body or explode, he bent his dark head, his tongue flicked lovingly over the deep pink tip and the world went crazy.

Writhing uncontrollably against him, she put her arms round his neck, pulled his head down to hers, and dazedly realised, to her utter relief, that he wasn't going to hold back—*couldn't* hold back any longer. He didn't care how much she touched him, she was free to run her hands over and over the strong curves of his back, his shoulder blades, down and down to his waist, up again to the line where his neck was brushed by the curling thickness of his hair, sliding adoringly over his damp, silky skin.

And as her hands moved with incredible, fast-growing boldness, his mouth found hers, fastened over it with fierce hunger, forced her to open up to him with a total lack of inhibition as he explored every last sweet corner, claiming it for his own. She couldn't stop him, she was way, way past the point where she even wanted to stop him. If this was a dream, then she could do whatever she wanted, and right now there was only one thing she craved above everything else. She wanted this man, her husband, to make love to her.

Then through the torrent of delight came the first faint murmur of unease. That plane crash had had so many dreadful consequences. Had he at last really been able to put all of it behind him, was he free of its curse?

Somehow, through the roar of raw desire, Jareth must have sensed her brief moment of hesitation. He raised his head, his eyes glittered darkly in the moonlight as he stared down at her.

'What is it?' he said hoarsely.

Sophie licked her dry lips.

'Is it—I mean, are you all right now?' she murmured anxiously.

The severe lines of his mouth relaxed into the shadow of a smile.

'Do you mean am I cured?' he asked huskily. His fingers threaded their way through her hair, he stared down into her eyes as he swiftly, without any warning, moved his body so that his weight was crushing down on her, imprinting his male outline on her from head to toe. She closed her eyes as she registered all the heady details, the firm ribcage that crushed the soft delicacy of her breasts, the flatness of his stomach, the potent strength of his thighs—and above all, like a living link between them, his unashamed arousal, fierce and demanding, shocking her with its forcefulness.

A wave of faintness swept over her, she gazed up at him through blurred eyes.

'Do you think that I'm cured, my sweet Sophie?' he challenged softly.

She was melting away, she could feel her bones dissolving, her flesh turning molten, until there was nothing left of her except a small burning core which ached for some kind of fulfilment which she could only hazily guess at. Wondering if any part of her still really existed, she lifted one arm, stared blankly at the hand which wavered in front of her, and saw the gold band on her finger as it glinted dully in the moonlight.

'I'm not awake,' she muttered feverishly. 'I know I'm not awake.'

Jareth's eyes instantly flared.

'Oh yes, my lady, you *are* awake,' he reminded her a little roughly. 'And I'm most certainly awake.' He seized hold of her hand, touched the gold ring as if it were some kind of talisman. 'You asked me if I were cured,' he reminded her thickly. 'Yes, I am, you know I am. But now I've got another kind of sickness. I want to make love to my wife!'

And that was like a physical blow to the face. The game of make-believe fell to pieces all around her, there could be no more hiding behind a wall of pretence, telling herself that it didn't matter what happened because none of this was real. And in the place of pleasure came a storm of guilt. Guilt because she was betraying David, betraying all her own principles and loyalties. And above all, guilt because she'd *wanted* this to happen. No use denying it any longer, this man who was now staring down at her so intently had some kind of hold over her. He'd said that he'd got some kind of sickness. Well, she'd got it, too. Something crazy was happening to her, she couldn't think of anyone but him, didn't want to be with anyone but him. All she wanted was to stay with him for ever and ever, utterly content never to leave his side.

But it was impossible. Drearily she acknowledged that fact to herself, feeling a desolate ache dragging at her bones as she struggled to find the strength to pull away from him.

She closed her eyes so that she wouldn't have to look at his face.

'I'm not your wife,' she muttered in a low, dull voice.

'Oh, but you are!' he responded, a hint of savagery creeping into his tone now. 'Damn it, Sophie, open your eyes and look at me!' As her eyelids flickered upwards, she caught the full force of his gaze as it bore down on her. 'No matter how much you might hate the thought of it, you're my legal wife. You belong to me,' he told her tautly.

Despair crept through her. Didn't he understand? She *wanted* to belong to him, wanted it so desperately she would have sold her soul to make it come true. But it just wasn't possible. She'd given her promise to David, he was waiting for her, she couldn't just pretend he didn't even exist.

'I belong to David,' she whispered, and experienced a flash of pure terror as she saw the darkness that swept over his face.

'You've no right to do this to me, Sophie,' he accused tautly, and she flinched as she heard the dangerous tension in his voice. 'No woman has the right to do what you've done tonight. Teasing is one thing. Leading a man on this far is something else again.'

She stared up at him with eyes that were huge and dark.

'What are you going to do?' she whispered. 'Force me? You could, you know, you're a lot stronger than I am.'

'Right now, I wish I was capable of it,' Jareth threw back at her furiously. 'I've certainly never come closer to it in my entire life. But contrary to what you might think, I'm not a violent man. Rape isn't my scene, in my book pleasure's something to be shared, not snatched. All the same, I wouldn't recommend that you try this on with David. He might have an entirely different point of view!'

As he finished speaking, he wrenched himself away from her. Then he slid off the bed and pulled on his shirt.

'Where—where are you going?' Sophie asked in a low, shaken voice.

'Going?' he repeated mockingly. 'I'm going nowhere, my dear wife. This is our wedding night, remember? The good Father would be rather suspicious in the morning if he found out your new husband had disappeared halfway through the night!'

She could just see his dark shadow as he moved around the room. Then she heard a faint creak as he flung himself down into the wooden chair, and knew that he was sitting there staring broodingly at the black velvet of the sky outside the window.

Trying not to make a sound, she pulled her nightdress straps back into place with trembling fingers, silently cursed the stupid, stupid whim that had made her put it on in the first place. Then she lay very still. The only sounds she could hear were the thudding of her heart and Jareth's too-fast breathing as he fought to quell the demons of desire that she'd set loose to torment him tonight.

The night seemed to last for ever. Neither of them slept, nor spoke or even moved. By the time the first pale glimmer of early morning light began to filter through the window, Sophie's entire body ached with tension. She stayed huddled under the quilt, though; she didn't want to have to leave the warm safety of the bed, see Jareth's face, hear his scathing tone of voice when he eventually spoke to her.

When she finally heard him moving around the room, she risked opening one eye, and shuddered a little as she saw the grim expression that shadowed his features. Although she hadn't made a sound, an instant later he turned to her, his gaze so remote that he seemed a total stranger.

'You'd better get up and dressed,' he said in a flat tone.

'It's still early,' she mumbled.

His blue eyes flashed ominously.

'Get packed and ready to leave. I don't want to have to stay here one moment longer than we have to.'

Sophie blinked nervously.

'But—where are we going?'

'I'm going to take you to Hajjar,' he answered, his face now totally unreadable. 'That's what you want, isn't it? To be reunited with David?'

She briefly closed her eyes. Right now, it was the very last thing on earth she wanted. She knew now only too well what she really wanted—also knew that she couldn't have it, that it was way, way out of her reach.

'Yes, of course it's what I want,' she lied in an utterly tired, utterly defeated voice.

Jareth threw a quick glance at her, for a moment she thought she saw puzzlement, even a spark of vivid curiosity, flicker deep in his eyes. Then she was sure she was mistaken, his features still wore that frighteningly withdrawn look, his gaze once again became deliberately blank.

As he finished stacking their belongings into a neat pile, she took advantage of the fact that his back was turned to her and slipped out of bed, hurriedly pulled on some clothes. Finding a comb, she dragged it through her hair, for some reason hating its black colour even more than usual this morning. Perhaps because it was a too-accurate reflection of her mood, she decided as she twisted it into a tight plait so that the long, dark strands would be out of her sight.

She completed her packing in silence, then stood stiffly by the window, staring down at the street below with unseeing eyes. She hated this place, absolutely hated it! If only someone would wave a magic wand and spirit her a way to—away to where? she asked herself with a touch of despair. A few days ago, that would have been such an easy question to answer. Away to David, of course. Now she was so confused, so emotionally mixed-up, that she wasn't sure that was the answer any longer. Home to England? To her parents, who would pamper and spoil her, try to soothe away all the pain?

Yet although she loved them dearly, somehow during these last few weeks she had finally outgrown them. She wasn't a little girl any longer, to have all her hurts taken care of by someone else. Somehow she had to learn how to deal with them herself, find away to plaster over the raw wounds until she could bear to live with them.

As they left the house and Jareth began to load up the camels, Sophie glanced up.

'Shouldn't we say goodbye to Father Donoghue?'

Jareth paused briefly.

'My guess is that Father Donoghue's rather under the weather this morning.'

'You mean he's got a hangover,' she said bluntly. Then she looked along the dusty street, at the mud-brick houses. 'And who can blame him?' she added with some bitterness. 'God, let's get out of here! I hate this place.'

In less than a quarter of an hour, they were leaving the town behind them, heading towards Hajjar.

I should be feeling really happy, Sophie told herself silently as the camels plodded along. This is what I wanted from the very beginning, for Jareth to take me to David. At last I've got my wish, everything's going exactly as I originally planned it. So why do I feel so damned miserable? Why can't I see more than a few yards in front of me because my eyes are blurred with all these stupid tears?

She stared at the shimmering outline of Jareth's straight back as he rode in front of her, and felt as if she were going quietly insane.

Everything will be all right again when I finally see David, she told herself a little wildly. It *has* to be all right.

Only she had an awful feeling that nothing was going to be all right ever again.

CHAPTER EIGHT

IT took them nearly four days to reach Hajjar. Fortunately, those days were mainly a blur in Sophie's memory. The journey was hard, the heat nearly unbearable at times. They could only travel early in the morning and late in the afternoon. Around midday, they would either camp under a tree or, if they couldn't find any shade, rig up a makeshift shelter with the blankets.

On the third day they encountered the *haboob*, the fierce desert wind which blew from the north. It brought with it a fine mist of sand that covered everything in a white veil, turning the landmarks into pale, ghostly shadows. There was nothing they could do except stop and huddle in the lee of the camels, with a blanket pulled right over their heads to try and find some protection against the fine, choking sand which blew into every nook and cranny.

For Sophie, every second was an agony, she was starkly aware of Jareth's body pressed hard against hers as they sheltered together from the penetrating wind. It brought all sorts of memories surging to the surface, memories which she had been grimly determined to forget. As for Jareth himself, she had no idea what he was thinking, what he was feeling. He seemed to have withdrawn right inside himself, and only spoke to her when it was absolutely necessary. Even then, his conversation was polite and strictly formal. They might have been two strangers who had only just met.

It was evening before the *haboob* finally died down,

and the moon was already rising like a pale yellow balloon into the dark velvet sky. In the distance, lightning was flashing with dazzling brilliance as a distant storm broke over the mountains. There was a subtle hint of menace in the air, a brooding quality which seemed reflected in the man beside her, a pent-up tension which could so easily explode with all the force of a thunderclap. Sophie shivered convulsively, told herself that it was only the chill of the evening, and yet knew that she was lying. It was Jareth Kingsley who was causing this cascade of goose-pimples across her skin.

Yet without Jareth, she knew she would never make it to Hajjar—to David. He was a constant source of strength, he never seemed to run out of energy, endurance, courage.

Even so, as their journey progressed, she found herself fervently wishing that he was a hundred, a thousand miles away. Although he kept up that almost chillingly remote attitude towards her, he was still physically *there*; she couldn't open her eyes in the morning without seeing his lean figure, she couldn't meet his gaze without being filled with wonder all over again at the sheer vividness of his eyes, their extraordinary depth of colour. It was like a subtle form of torture, and by the end of the four days her nerves were so ragged that she felt as if they were about to fly apart.

Then they were at last approaching Hajjar, and she became conscious of a curious sense of dread creeping up on her. This was ridiculous! she lectured herself severely. She was going to meet David—*David*, not some complete stranger. There was absolutely nothing to be nervous about. Yet the feeling stubbornly refused to go away, in fact it just kept getting stronger until it was hard to stop the panic from running completely out of control.

Hajjar turned out to be like most of the other small towns they had passed through, dusty streets, mud-brick houses, people noisily buying and selling their wares in the market square, which smelt of fruit and spices, perfume and oil, and the rich scent of new leather. There were herds of camels passing through on their way to more distant markets, many of them laden with charcoal and gum arabic, and the sounds and aromas were rather overwhelming.

A couple of times, Jareth stopped and asked for directions, and on the third time a dark face became instantly alert when David's name was mentioned. There was much pointing into the distance and a spate of rapid Arabic followed as detailed instructions were given on how to reach David's house.

'It should only take a few minutes to get there,' Jareth told Sophie as the conversation finally came to an end. 'It's apparently only a couple of streets away.'

Sophie's stomach gave an odd lurch, and she had an awful impulse to turn round and just run and run. Instead, she somehow pulled her shattered nerves together and urged her camel along after Jareth, who was already moving off.

Soon—far too soon, it seemed to her—they came to a halt in front of a house that was a little larger than the others around it.

'This should be it,' Jareth told her, in a cool, even tone that gave her no clue whatsoever to his inner feelings.

Her legs feeling horribly unsteady, she slid down from her camel. Then she just stood there, staring at the door.

A moment later, to her surprise, Jareth also dismounted.

'I thought you'd be leaving as soon as you'd delivered me to David,' she said in a small voice.

He gave a slightly grim smile.

'You seem to be forgetting that there are a couple of rather important things to be dealt with before you're free to go ahead with your marriage to David.'

Involuntarily, Sophie glanced down at the gold ring on her finger and caught herself remembering what a perfect fit it was. Then she made an effort to be more practical and businesslike.

'Oh yes, the annulment,' she said, somehow managing to keep her voice almost casual.

'The annulment,' he agreed. 'We've got to come to some sort of arrangement before I leave.'

She swallowed hard.

'What—what sort of arrangement?'

'That's something that we'll discuss later,' he told her smoothly. 'Right now, you probably can't wait to rush over and meet David.'

'Yes. Yes, of course.' She hoped he couldn't hear the lack of conviction in her voice. After taking half a dozen steps forward, she glanced back. 'Aren't you coming with me?'

To her dismay, Jareth shook his head.

'I'll take a walk around the town for an hour or two, stretch my legs and find somewhere to leave the camels. You know the old saying,' he added rather tersely. 'Two's company, three's a crowd.'

'Oh, but——' Abruptly, she stopped. If she blurted out that she didn't *want* to meet David by herself, Jareth was going to be highly suspicious. Anyway, there was nothing to be scared of, it was only David she was going to meet.

The man you're going to marry, added an insidious voice inside her head. Then she stared down at her hand again. But I'm already married, she reminded herself silently. Oh God, what a mess! What an awful, awful mess.

She turned round—and felt her nerve-ends give a small flutter of dismay. Jareth had already disappeared from sight. She was completely on her own.

Legs visibly shaking, she somehow managed to stumble across the last few yards to the house. Then she lifted her hand, hesitated one last time before forcing herself to knock firmly on the door.

Almost immediately, the door swung open quietly. Then her pounding heart quietened a little as she saw not David standing there, but a young Arab girl, staring at her with inquisitive black eyes.

Sophie struggled with her Arabic.

'Does Mr Stanton—David Stanton—live here?' she finally managed to get out.

'I can speak English,' the Arab girl said gravely.

'Thank heavens for that!' breathed Sophie with relief. 'Have I got the right house? Do you know a David Stanton?'

'Yes, he lives here,' nodded the girl. 'He is the one who taught me English. My name is Zahra.'

Sophie stared at her with a little more interest. The girl not only had ravishing eyes, she was also startlingly pretty. She wasn't very old, of course, probably only in her mid to late teens, but Sophie knew that was when these dark-haired, dark-eyed girls were at the peak of their beauty. After that, unless they were very lucky, the heat and the hard life they led began to take its toll. Sophie found herself hoping that Zahra would find someone who would take good care of her, preserve that dazzling prettiness for a few more years.

'Do you live here?' she asked curiously.

Zahra instantly looked shocked.

'Of course not. I come during the day to cook for David and to keep his house clean and tidy.'

She pronounced David's name in an enchanting way, and at the same time those liquid black eyes softened a little. Before Sophie had time to jump to any conclusions, though, a familiar voice called out from inside the house.

'Who is it, Zahra?'

Sophie's pulse rate rocketed. For the briefest of instances, Jareth ceased to dominate her mind. *This* was the man she had travelled all these thousands of miles to be with.

'It is a lady to see you, David,' called back Zahra.

A couple of seconds later, a man of medium height appeared behind Zahra. Sophie's gaze ran eagerly over his face; she saw a pleasant-looking man with a mop of slightly untidy fair hair, pale blue eyes that were somehow just an ordinary blue, not like——

Swiftly, she put a brake on her treacherous thoughts, absolutely forbade them to make any more comparisons.

'Hallo, David,' she said with a nervous smile.

He stared at her blankly.

'Good morning,' he replied politely.

Sophie blinked, wondered if this was some kind of joke. Then she remembered that David didn't play jokes. In fact, he didn't really have much of a sense of humour. Then she suddenly realised what she looked like with her dyed black hair and wearing the outlandish Arab clothes. He didn't recognise her!

Hardly flattering, but perfectly understandable, she tried to convince herself. Her own mother probably wouldn't know her if she walked in the door looking like this!

'It's me,' she prompted, with a slightly anxious flutter

of her lashes. 'Sophie.'

David stared at her very hard for several seconds.

'Sophie?' he echoed incredulously at last. Then recognition slowly filtered into his pale eyes. 'My God, it *is* you!' he went on in a shaken voice. 'What on earth are you doing here? And your hair,' he said almost in horror, 'your beautiful hair! Oh, Sophie, what's happened to it?'

She laughed slightly unsteadily.

'It's a rather long story. Can I come in?'

'Of course, of course,' he said, as if it had only just dawned on him that they were still standing in the doorway. 'Zahra, would you be kind enough to make us some tea?'

He led Sophie into a room that was furnished in a rather unhappy mixture of English and Arab styles, gestured to her to sit down on a low sofa piled with brightly coloured cushions while he sank into a shabby armchair.

'You're the very last person I ever expected to see standing on my doorstep,' he admitted frankly.

'There were times when I thought I wouldn't make it,' she confessed. 'But luckily I—well, I met someone who finally got me here safely.'

'Thank God you found a good guide,' he told her soberly. 'The desert's no place for a girl travelling alone. Heavens, when I think of all the things that might have happened to you——' he paused, gave a small shudder, and Sophie took advantage of the slight pause to plunge on hurriedly.

'There's a lot more to it than that, though, I'm afraid. You see, the man who brought me here——'

'Ah, here comes the tea,' David interrupted her as Zahra came in carrying a small tray.

Sophie had to suppress a small smile. David was so

endearingly old-fashioned in some ways. Even though they were in the middle of the desert, everything still had to stop for afternoon tea!

As she drank her tea, she was aware of him staring at her in slight dismay, his gaze sliding away from her face every time she raised her eyes to meet his.

'Sorry,' he apologised at last, 'it's just that I can't get used to you with black hair. What on earth made you dye it that awful colour?'

'I ran into a bit of trouble with one of the local sheiks,' she explained ruefully. 'He took rather a fancy to me— I'd never have got away from him if it hadn't been for Jareth. Anyway, some of his men were looking for me, so Jareth decided I'd better dye my hair, to make it more difficult for them to find me, and——'

'Jareth?' interrupted David, with a frown. 'Who's Jareth?'

'He's the man I told you about earlier, the one who brought me here.'

David's face changed perceptibly, his frown deepened.

'Then you didn't have an Arab guide?' he questioned a little sharply.

Sophie wriggled on the sofa rather nervously.

'Well—actually, no. I did travel with some Arab camel-herders for a while, but then I got a fever, and that was when they dumped me on Jareth.'

'But who *is* this Jareth?' insisted David. 'And what's he doing in this part of the world? We hardly see a European from one year to the next out here.'

Quite suddenly, Sophie didn't want to go into all the very personal details of the tragedy that had driven Jareth to the isolation of the desert. It was too private, she knew he would hate it if everyone knew what he had been through these past few months.

'His name's Jareth Kingsley. And he's just travelling around,' she said with deliberate vagueness, fervently hoping that David wouldn't press for more details. 'He was making his way up to Egypt, I think, and he very kindly made a detour so he could bring me here, to Hajjar.'

'That's quite a sizeable detour,' David pointed out in a quiet voice.

Sophie sighed.

'I suppose I'd better tell you the rest of it,' she said with resignation. 'I got into another spot of trouble a few days back. I lost my passport and papers.'

'They're very strict about having the proper documents out here,' commented David, his face instantly creasing into a worried frown. 'So what did you do? You couldn't possibly have got duplicates, not in that short time.'

She cleared her throat nervously. Now she was getting to the difficult bit, and she could feel a film of dampness breaking out on her palms.

'No, I couldn't get duplicates,' she agreed in a small voice. 'And I knew I was in a lot of trouble if I couldn't find someone who'd be legally responsible for me.'

The first glimmerings of suspicion began to shadow David's pale eyes.

'Out here, there's only one person who's considered legally responsible for a woman, and that's her husband,' he said slowly.

'Er—yes, that's right,' Sophie nodded with extreme apprehension. 'That's why I had to get married.'

The look of shock on his face sent a great surge of guilt through her. Oh, why had she done it? David would never forgive her, never.

'Married?' he echoed disbelievingly, all the colour abruptly draining from his face. 'You're *married*?'

'There was no other way! If I hadn't gone through with it, I'd probably have been deported,' she explained frantically.

He ran his fingers shakily through his hair.

'But Sophie, we were engaged, we were going to be married when I came back to England!'

'Yes, I know,' she said miserably. 'And I'm sorry, David, I really am, but I just didn't have any choice. I didn't *want* to get married.'

Didn't you? mocked a sly little voice inside her head. Horrified, she tried to ignore it.

David was sighing heavily.

'I don't really understand any of this,' he confessed. 'All right, so you'd have been deported. What was so dreadful about that? You could have gone back to England and waited for me there, and we'd have been married at the end of the year, as we planned.'

'And I might also have spent several weeks in jail before I was deported,' Sophie told him almost tearfully. 'You know what this country's like, David, you've got to admit that was a distinct possibility.'

His eyes became shadowed.

'Yes, that was a possibility,' he admitted. 'But Sophie, to get married——'

At the haggard look on his face, Sophie felt totally stricken. How could she have done this to a fine man like David? Oh God, she'd do anything to take that hurt look from his face. She resolved to spend the rest of her life trying to make it up to him.

She drew in a deep, unsteady breath and was about to explain it all over again, somehow try and force him to understand the panic that had driven her to such a desperate measure, when Zahra glided quietly back into the room.

'There is a man waiting outside,' she announced. 'He

says his name is Jareth Kingsley.'

'Ah yes, the man who brought you here,' David recalled, a little absently. 'Ask him to come in, Zahra.'

Sophie felt a sudden quiver in all her nerve-ends. Then she went very still as Jareth walked into the room.

David stood up to greet him, and Sophie found herself staring at the two men as they stood opposite one another. It was so hard not to make comparisons. Jareth was taller, leaner, his eyes that deep, beautiful shade of blue, his face so vividly alive, his body—Sophie shivered. No, she mustn't think of that supple, scarred body, the pleasure it could inflict, the strong needs that drove it. That path was a crazy helter-skelter ride to total insanity.

The two men shook hands, then Jareth glanced briefly in her direction.

'I assume that Miss Carlton has told you everything that's happened these last few days?' he said, turning back to David.

'I know that she's no longer "Miss Carlton",' David responded in an uncharacteristically tense voice.'

'Er—I didn't have time to tell him quite *everything*,' Sophie interrupted, glancing uneasily from one man to the other. 'David, I didn't tell you who I married.'

David's face became even more drawn.

'No, you didn't,' he agreed.

'She married me,' Jareth cut in quietly.

The atmosphere instantly became unpleasantly fraught, as if an electric storm were hovering directly overhead.

'Sophie, why don't you wait outside?' suggested Jareth, in that same low but reasonable voice. 'There are obviously several things David and I have to discuss, and it would probably be much easier if you weren't here.'

Glad to have the chance to escape, Sophie fled from the room, heard David's voice rising sharply even before she had closed the door, then Jareth's calm, steadying tones. Not wanting to hear a single word of what they were saying, she ran towards the back of the house, eventually burst through a half-open door and into a small kitchen.

Zahra looked up, startled.

'What is it?' she asked anxiously. 'Has something happened to David?'

The girl's instant concern immediately registered on Sophie's quick brain, she stared at Zahra with new understanding.

'No, nothing's happened to David,' she said slowly at last. 'He's fine.'

Zahra relaxed and went back to kneading the dough on the table in front of her.

'Will you and your husband be staying long?' she asked in a friendly voice.

'My husband?' repeated Sophie confusedly.

Zahra glanced at the gold ring on Sophie's finger.

'The tall man who arrived a short time ago,' she said, with a small nod of her delicate head. 'He is your husband, is he not?'

'Well—yes, he is,' Sophie admitted reluctantly. She was about to launch into the complicated explanation of the truth, then abruptly stopped. It was pretty obvious that Zahra was very fond of David—perhaps more than just fond. It wasn't going to cheer her up to learn that Sophie was just waiting for an annulment so that she and David could get married. No, there would be plenty of time later for all the difficult explanations. Let Zahra keep her peace of mind for a little while longer.

She ran her fingers absently through the dusty strands of her hair, then tapped her foot restlessly on the floor.

Oh, it was impossible to just stand still, she needed to
get involved in some physical activity that would take
her mind off things.

Inspiration struck.

'Zahra, I'd like to wash my hair,' she announced. 'Is
there enough water?'

Zahra looked doubtful.

'There is still half a bucketful left from the water the
boy fetched this morning. Would that be enough?'

Sophie shook her head.

'Definitely not.'

'If you give the boy a couple of coins, he'll fetch as
much as you like from the well. He only lives next door.
Shall I call him?'

'Yes, please,' Sophie nodded.

Zahra abandoned her dough and went to fetch the
boy, Yusif, who was about eleven or twelve and thin and
wiry.

The first bucket of water arrived within a few
minutes. Sophie had already fetched the large bottle of
shampoo from her carefully chosen supply of essential
beauty aids that she had got packed into her toilet bag.
The water was cold, but she didn't care. It would take
too long to wait for it to heat up on the ancient wood-
burning stove that stood in one corner. She dunked her
head into the bucket, and when her hair was thoroughly
wet, rubbed in a large handful of shampoo.

To her relief, the black dye instantly started to pour
out. She heard Zahra give a sharp exclamation of
surprise as the water turned the colour of Indian ink,
then the Arab girl swiftly ordered Yusif to fetch a couple
of extra buckets.

After that, the two girls worked hard on Sophie's
hair, rubbing in the shampoo, vigorously working the
lather through the long strands, rinsing and rinsing until

at last a pale glint of her own colour began to shine through.

As they stopped briefly for a breather, Zahra touched Sophie's hair in wonder.

'Such a colour!' she marvelled. 'Why ever did you dye it?'

'There was a sheik who liked it just a little too much,' Sophie said drily.

Zahra instantly nodded understandingly.

'There must be many men who would be willing to give a great many camels to possess a wife with hair like yours.'

'I don't think the sheik intended to give any camels at all,' Sophie told her, with a small grimace. 'He was a man used to taking what he wanted without making any payment for it at all. Jareth—my husband,' she added, feeling a twinge of pleasure and guilt as she said the word, 'he helped me to get away, then we dyed my hair so that the sheik wouldn't be able to find me.'

Zahra's dark head bobbed up and down wisely.

'It is good to have such a strong husband, who can protect you from men such as that sheik. You are very lucky.'

'Yes, I'm very lucky,' Sophie repeated. Then she dipped her head back into the bucket before Zahra could comment on the faint note of bitterness in her voice.

By the time the two girls had finally finished, Sophie's hair was back to its full glorious colour again. She towel-dried it on a long strip of cotton which Zahra provided, then began to comb it as Zahra went back to finish kneading her dough.

In the warmth of the kitchen, her hair was soon completely dry. She was just running the comb through the glossy apricot strands for the last time, getting a

strange, almost sensual delight from the sensation,
feeling a glow of pleasure from the knowledge that the
dye hadn't harmed it at all, when Jareth walked into the
kitchen.

His gaze fixed on her hair immediately, for several
long seconds he didn't seem able to talk.

'There are several things I have to say to you,' he got
out at last in a rather strained voice. 'Is there somewhere
we can talk in private?'

'There is a small courtyard through there,' Zahra told
them, pointing towards a door at the back of the
kitchen. 'No one else uses it, you will be quite alone.'

Walking on legs that felt distinctly weak, Sophie
followed him out into the late afternoon sunlight, found
herself standing in a tiny courtyard which was gently
shadowed by a spreading tree. She thought she saw
Zahra's hand in the few pots of straggling flowers which
brightened up the dusty corners. Then Jareth's shadow
fell over her and it was suddenly impossible to think of
anything but him.

I love this man so very much, she thought to herself in
amazement. And it seemed the most natural thing in the
world to love him, she couldn't imagine *not* loving him.
When had it happened? She wasn't sure. Ages ago, she
suspected. Perhaps even at that moment when she had
first opened her eyes and seen him sitting there beside
her and mistaken him for a bandit.

Part of her ached to tell him; the other part knew it
was useless. She was in David's house, she belonged to
David. Although her parents had been loving, they had
also been strict. She had had all the old-fashioned
principles drummed into her since birth, and at the top
of the list came loyalty. Once you'd given your word to
someone, you didn't break it simply because it wasn't
convenient any more. Hadn't she caused David enough

heartache and misery? And she'd made a solemn promise to herself that she would make it up to him once they were married.

But you're already married to this man, murmured an insidious little voice inside her head.

Oh, stop it, stop it! she screamed silently. I can't stand this any more!

She closed her eyes very tight for a moment, waiting for common sense to slowly prevail. All right, she reasoned drearily to herself at last, she might secretly long to stay married to Jareth, but it was time to face a few more unpalatable facts. He certainly didn't want to be married to *her*. Okay, so he'd wanted to make love to her. But on his own admission, it had been months since he'd touched a woman. Once all the old desires came surging back, probably any female would have done as long as she was reasonably attractive. And Sophie was under no illusions about her own looks. Even with her hair dyed black, she had never entirely lost the beauty which had dazzled men ever since she'd reached adolescence.

She looked up, saw that Jareth was looking at her with unusual gentleness.

'Daydreaming?' he said with unexpected perception.

Don't let him suspect, Sophie warned herself frantically. Don't ever, ever let him suspect.

'Of David,' she lied, fighting desperately hard to keep her own voice steady.

The gentleness instantly left his blue eyes and his face took on the old familiar blank expression.

'We had a long talk, David and I,' he told her distantly, 'and I've managed to convince him that our marriage was only intended to be temporary, that we were never husband and wife except on paper. I'm returning to England as soon as I leave here. I'll make arrangements about the annulment as soon as I'm back home again, so you should be hearing from my solicitors in due course.'

'What will happen in the meantime?' she asked uncertainly. 'What if some official comes round asking awkward questions?'

'You've got your marriage certificate,' he replied. 'That should be enough to keep them happy for a while.'

'Oh yes, I'll be able to produce a marriage certificate, but not a husband,' she retorted. 'Aren't they going to think that a bit funny?'

Jareth sighed.

'Sophie, stop making difficulties. All you've got to say is that I'm away on a business trip.'

'And do you really think that'll satisfy them?' she demanded.

A dark shadow crossed his face.

'What do you expect me to do? To stay here with you? Well, I can't!' he exploded. 'I can't,' he repeated in a quieter voice. He was silent for a moment, then he went on in a more controlled tone, 'I'll do everything I can to get you out of this mess, I promise you that. Once I'm back in England, I'll go and see all the appropriate people, get you duplicate copies of all your papers as soon as I can. I can't do more than that.'

'No, I know you can't,' she said, her own voice much more subdued now. Stubbornly, she ignored the painful ache that had begun to gnaw away deep inside her. 'Well, everything seems to be settled, then,' she said, making an effort to sound brisk and detached. 'When——' Her tone faltered alarmingly, she struggled hard to control it. 'When will you be leaving?'

'First thing in the morning. David insisted that I should stay overnight. It's too late to travel any further today.'

They both seemed to have run out of words. For the first time ever, there was an awkward silence between them. Jareth stirred restlessly, he seemed on the point of walking away. Then, as if he couldn't help himself, he lifted his hand and ran his fingertips slowly, almost reverently, across the shimmering waterfall of her hair.

'I'd forgotten how beautiful it was,' he muttered in a taut voice.

Then he wheeled round and quickly strode away, leaving her to stand there shaking helplessly.

The evening was an ordeal that stretched on and on, the three of them sitting down to a long, leisurely meal, neither of the men apparently noticing that Sophie hardly touched more than a mouthful of food. Then there was the awful effort of trying to follow the casual conversation that followed, of somehow making the right mumbled comment at the appropriate moments. But it was even worse when they finally went to bed, because then Sophie had so much time to lie awake in the darkness, trying to come to terms with the fact that, in the morning, Jareth would be gone.

It was impossible, she couldn't do it. Stupid, really, when she'd known him such a short time, but she felt as if he'd been a part of her life for ever, and she couldn't imagine what it would be like not to have him there arguing with her, teasing her—making love to her.

She shuddered, turned over, and buried her hot face in the pillow. Don't even think about it! she ordered herself fiercely. Don't think about it, and then perhaps you'll be able to stand it. It's David you're going to marry, David you're going to spend the rest of your life with, *David*——

And to her horror, the thought totally appalled her. With a small moan, she closed her eyes so tight that they hurt, and prayed hard for the oblivion of sleep. And someone, somewhere, at last took pity on her and the darkness finally swallowed her up.

She woke up just after dawn, and lay in bed for a while feeling utterly exhausted, as if she'd never had those couple of hours of restless sleep. Then she became aware of voices outside the window, heard the distinctive snort of a camel.

Sliding out of bed, she padded over to the window, shivering slightly in the early morning chill. Then, as she glanced out, she forgot all about being cold, and her body became rigid as she saw Jareth expertly loading the camel with his few bundles of possessions.

He was leaving! And without even saying goodbye.

With frantic haste, Sophie pulled on jeans and a T-shirt, not even bothering with shoes but flying downstairs on bare feet. Bursting out of the house, she then just stood there in the dusty road, suddenly shy, awkward, not knowing what to say, only knowing that she couldn't let him leave without some kind of a last goodbye.

She didn't even hear David bustle out of the house behind her.

'You're up early,' he said in some surprise. Then his pale eyes flickered appreciatively. 'But you look gorgeous, darling,' he went on, and he bent his head to kiss her.

At the last moment she turned away, his mouth merely brushed her cheek, and even then she had to fight the impulse to raise her hand and wipe away that brief touch of his lips.

Then she raised her head, saw Jareth watching them with a tight, intense expression. Realising that she had to play this charade out to the end, she turned to David, but couldn't bring herself to kiss him, though she did somehow manage to put her arm lightly around his waist.

His body felt curiously soft, almost flabby. With a sense of shock, Sophie realised she'd become accustomed to Jareth's lean hardness, the stimulating sensation of powerful muscles under supple skin.

After only a couple of seconds, she edged away again, and was grateful when David made no attempt to move after her but instead went to help Jareth load the last of his bundles on to the camel.

Then Jareth was lithely climbing up on to the camel's back and the moment was actually here—he was leaving, and she found that her throat and chest had seized up and she couldn't say anything at all. As she gazed up at him, for the briefest of instances their eyes met, and that vivid blue gaze rested intently on her face. Then he wheeled the camel round, urging the animal forward with unnecessary vigour, so that it broke almost immediately into a fast lope.

'Now why on earth is he setting off at that speed?' remarked David in some surprise.

Sophie wasn't even listening, her gaze was fixed blindly on the tall, departing figure.

Let him look back, she prayed silently. Oh, please, *please* let him look back just once!

But Jareth's back remained rigid, his head held tensely high as if his neck muscles had locked into that position.

Then he reached the point where the road wound out of sight, and all of a sudden Sophie couldn't see him any more.

A wave of utter panic swept over her, her legs quivered with the urge to run after him, find some way, *any* way, of stopping him from going. Her body was actually poised on the point of flight when David's hand descended on her shoulder.

'Well, he's gone,' he said with some satisfaction. 'We're on our own now.'

All her muscles abruptly slumped defeatedly. It had been just a fantasy, she'd never have been able to catch him. And even if she had, what could she have said, what could she have done to make him stay?

She wanted desperately to shake off the heavy weight of David's hand, but somehow forced herself to endure it.

'Yes, he's gone,' she echoed dully.

Then she turned and followed him back into the house. And when she stared at her reflection in the mirror a little later, she knew that something inside her had just shrivelled up and died.

CHAPTER NINE

THE next few days were so awful that Sophie had no idea how she ever got through them. The only thing that made them even vaguely bearable was the rather surprising fact that David left her very much alone. Apart from a brief peck on the cheek occasionally, there was virtually no physical contact between them. And during the day, when Zahra was around, he made no attempt to touch her at all.

As some of the numb pain at last began to wear off, she discovered something else. She was bored—completely, screamingly bored. David's work absorbed him totally, he was out for hours at a time, and even when he returned, his conversation seemed to centre solely on what he had accomplished so far at his small school, what his plans were for the future. Guiltily, Sophie told herself she ought to be interested, she tried really hard to get involved, even suggesting to David that she could take one or two classes to try and relieve his crippling work load. He had reluctantly turned down her suggestion, though. Her Arabic wasn't good enough yet, he explained. And anyway, it would be some time yet before she fully understood these people, she wouldn't know how to tailor the lessons so that they fitted into their culture and would be relevant to their working life and home environment.

It made sense, she knew he was right, and yet somehow she still resented the fact that he was keeping her out of such a large and important part of his life. She had marched up to her room, slammed the door and flung herself down on the bed in frustration. It wasn't just that David seemed to be shutting her out of his life. Over the past couple of weeks, he seemed to have developed an infuriating tendency to treat her as if she were little more than a child, someone who needed to be protected from the squalor and harshness of everyday life in this remote desert town.

It was driving her mad!

She couldn't even keep herself busy with mundane household chores. Zahra took care of everything, the cooking, shopping, cleaning, laundry; there was absolutely nothing for her to do. Nor would Zahra allow her to help, she'd even looked rather shocked when Sophie had suggested it. This was what David paid her to do, how could she take his money if someone else was doing half the work?

Time dragged by, each day finding her more bored, more frustrated, more bewildered. What was she doing here, in this efficiently-run household where there seemed to be no place for her, no useful function she could perform? And where was the man she had known in London? The gentle lover she remembered had disappeared, in his place was a man who worked too hard, who seemed almost obsessively absorbed in the school he had founded, and apparently had little time for—or interest in—anything else.

Several days later, when David was at the school and Zahra was out shopping, there was a sharp rap at the door. Sophie opened it, then felt her stomach turn right over as she saw the man in a police uniform standing outside.

'Am I addressing Sophia Carlton?' he enquired in a very formal tone, speaking excellent if slightly stilted English.

'Yes, you are,' she somehow managed to croak.

'We have been trying to trace you for quite some time,' the police officer told her, his gaze fixed sternly on her face.

Visions of being marched straight off to jail flittered through Sophie's panic-stricken head; she started to shake, wanting Jareth here so very badly that she actually whispered his name under her breath. He'd be able to get her out of this, he had always rescued her in the past.

Only he wasn't here now, no one was. She was alone with this stern-faced police officer, who was already reaching into his pocket. Oh God, what was he getting out? A warrant for her arrest?

'We have found some papers that I believe belong to you,' he told her. 'Passport, travel documents, visas—surely you realised they were missing?'

Sophie stared at him in dazed disbelief. Her papers? They'd found her papers?

'Where—where did you get them?' she stuttered.

'They were found at the Badr oasis,' he replied, with a small frown. 'I believe you camped there overnight, several weeks ago. You were very fortunate, they were picked up by one of the desert nomads who then handed them in to us, thinking that there might be some reward.'

Something in his tone of voice made her realise what he expected from her. She hurried back into the house, returning a minute later with a handful of notes, which she discreetly handed to him.

'I'm very grateful to that nomad,' she said politely. 'Would you be kind enough to see that he receives this small token of my thanks?'

The money was slid equally discreetly into the officer's inner pocket, and Sophie was absolutely certain it would never reach the man who had actually found and handed in her papers.

'You realise that the loss of such papers should have been reported immediately? That it is a serious offence to travel around this country without the proper documents?' the officer lectured her sternly. Then his dark features relaxed slightly. 'However, since the papers have now been found and safely returned to you, I am prepared to let you off with just a warning this time. Please be more careful in future, though, or you could find yourself in very serious trouble. Good day to you.'

He turned round and marched off, leaving her to gaze dazedly at the documents she now held in her hands. She was free to come and go again, as she pleased. She was free——

Her elation faded away. No, she wasn't, there were still ties that held her here. She owed it to David to make one last effort to make it work between them.

She was waiting for him when he returned from the school later that afternoon.

'I've got a proposition to put to you,' she said, sitting down opposite him. 'I need something to *do*, David. If you won't let me help you in the school, why don't you get rid of Zahra and let me run the house for you?'

David immediately looked shocked.

'Get rid of Zahra?' he echoed. 'But that's impossible!'

'Why?' she asked reasonably.

'Well—you've been waited on hand and foot all your life, you wouldn't have the slightest idea what to do, we'd be living in complete chaos,' he answered in a rather flustered voice.

'That's nonsense,' Sophie said calmly. 'What do you think I am, a complete idiot? Although I might well end up one if I've got to go on like this much longer,' she added. 'I'm stuck here day after day with nothing to do, no one to talk to. David, can't you understand what it's doing to me—to us?'

'Perhaps you should have stayed in England,' he said, with a light frown. 'This is no place for a girl like you. We could have been married when I returned home——'

'And when would that be?' she cut in. 'Only a couple of days ago, you were talking about signing a contract to stay out here for another two years!'

'It might mean postponing the wedding for a while,' he admitted. 'But we're both young, we can afford to wait.'

To her amazement, Sophie realised that he seemed almost relieved at the idea.

'And what if I don't want to wait?' she said slowly, studying his face very carefully now. 'What if I want to get married straightaway, David?'

He seemed strangely ill at ease.

'You're married already,' he reminded her. 'We've no choice except to wait.'

'My annulment could arrive any day now.' she persisted. 'And then I'll be free.'

David glanced edgily over his shoulder.

'Please keep your voice down,' he begged. 'Zahra might overhear. She doesn't know anything about—well, our personal problems. She thinks you're just staying here for a while until your husband returns.'

Sophie gaped at him in total astonishment.

'Who on earth told her that?' she demanded.

'Er—I did,' he admitted. 'I thought—well, I thought it would be best——'

'And what did you plan to tell her when we were finally married?' she interrupted slightly sarcastically.

His confusion grew by the second, colour began to creep into his face.

'I don't know——' he confessed, with a small, oddly helpless shrug.

Sophie slumped back in the chair. The truth was at last beginning to dawn on her, and she felt completely shattered by it. Why on earth hadn't she seen it before? She must have been completely blind! For a moment, she felt a wild desire to laugh rather hysterically. Instead, though, she somehow kept control of herself and stared straight at David.

'You don't want to marry me at all, do you?' she said, with unexpected calmness.

Instantly, he looked very indignant.

'Of course I do, Sophie, you know I do. I love you.'

She shook her head, feeling strangely sad. Her own reasons for coming here had been muddled and confused, but she wasn't the only one who had been deluded by what had happened in London. David, too, had been caught up in the same bright illusory dream. But reality, for both of them, was a very different kind of life—and not with each other.

'You don't love me,' she said quietly and with complete conviction. 'You love Zahra.'

From the totally bedazzled look on his face, she knew that he hadn't even realised it himself.

'I certainly do not!' he denied vehemently. 'Why, Zahra's an—an——'

'An Arab?' she finished for him. 'Of course she is. She's also young, pretty, and head over heels in love with you. And she's very intelligent, David—she'd be the perfect wife for you. You love these people, you know you do. And you've been doing marvellous work here. With you and Zahra working as a team, who knows what you might be able to accomplish?'

He still looked as if she'd just hit him with a sledgehammer.

'Zahra,' he murmured under his breath, dazedly.

'Think about it,' Sophie advised. 'Talk it over with Zahra herself. I'm going for a walk,' she went on, getting up. 'I'll be back in a couple of hours. By then you'd better have everything sorted out, because I've got a few decisions of my own to make.'

She left the house straightaway, then wandered around the town for ages, buying a few trinkets—souvenirs, she realised with a rueful smile, because she was in no doubt what David would eventually decide.

She had turned her back on Jareth because of a promise made a long time ago to a man whom, it turned out, she had hardly known at all. Now David didn't want her either, and she was left with nothing. All her fine plans lay in shattered pieces all around her, in just a few hours the direction of her life had changed yet again, and right now she didn't know where she was going.

Well, she decided with a wry shrug, it looked as if she was just going to have to make an all-out effort to pick up the pieces and start all over again. Only this time, she was determined things were going to be different. She was tired of drifting aimlessly through life, she had brains and she intended to use them. All right, so it might mean going on a training course of some kind, or trying several different jobs until she found one she liked and was good at. But at least she would have some kind of purpose, and it would keep her occupied.

And she had a feeling that was going to prove vitally important because, no matter how optimistically she tried to look at it, a shudder of apprehension still racked her every time she thought of the desperately bleak and empty future that now stretched ahead of her.

When she got back to England, the skies were grey and

a soft rain was falling. After the burning heat of the past few weeks, it was a wonderful sensation. Sophie held up her face and let the cool drops splash against her hot skin.

From the airport, she got a taxi to her cousin Kate's flat. Drooping with fatigue, she dumped her luggage on the doorstep and pressed the bell.

Kate opened it half a minute later.

'Sophie! What on earth are you doing here?' Kate peered round her. 'And where's Lawrence of Arabia? Or should I say David of Arabia?' she giggled.

'David's still in the Sahara, rather dazzled by the prospect of marrying a gorgeous little Arab girl,' Sophie replied briefly. 'Can I come in, Kate? I'm dog-tired, I feel as if I've been travelling for ever.'

Kate instantly pulled her inside and hustled her into the front room of the tiny flat.

'Stretch out on the sofa and have a rest,' she instructed. 'I'll make some coffee.'

'Have you heard from my parents?' asked Sophie slightly anxiously, kicking off her shoes and flopping down on to the sofa with a sigh of relief.

'They've rung a couple of times,' Kate called back through the open kitchen door. 'I told them you were staying with friends who weren't on the phone, but that you'd ring them as soon as you could. That wasn't exactly a lie, was it?' she added slightly guiltily, reappearing briefly in the doorway. 'After all, you were with David, and he *was* a friend. At least, I reckoned he was at the time, I didn't realise he was just another male rat.'

'It wasn't David's fault,' said Sophie tiredly.

'Of course it was,' insisted Kate staunchly. 'After all, he asked you to marry him. Why else would you have gone rushing off on that mad journey?'

Sophie could hardly remember how it had begun, only how it had ended. She closed her eyes for a couple of seconds.

'My parents—they're all right?' she asked eventually.

'They're fine,' Kate assured her. 'Worrying about you, as usual. Your mother said to tell you that a cold spell was forecast and to be sure to remember to wear a thick vest.'

Sophie began to laugh, but then it choked in her throat and somehow she was crying instead, the tears pouring down her face and dripping off her chin.

Kate hurried to fetch a couple of large hankies.

'Here,' she said, stuffing them into Sophie's hand. 'Have a good cry, you'll probably feel much better afterwards.'

'I don't think I'm ever going to feel better again,' snuffled Sophie miserably.

'Of course you will,' declared Kate firmly. 'First, I'm going to put a large slug of brandy in your coffee. Then when you've drunk it, we'll have a long chat about this rat, David. Honestly, Sophie, from what you've told me, I think you're far better off without him. After all, who wants a husband who wants to spend the rest of his life in the Sahara?'

'Not me,' agreed Sophie, blowing her nose hard.

While Kate fetched the coffee, Sophie lifted the phone and dialled her parents' number. When she heard her mother's voice at the other end, it was a couple of minutes before she could say anything at all.

Her mother was full of worried questions after not hearing from her for so long, but there was so much Sophie couldn't say; she just wasn't ready to confide yet. When she finally had control of her voice, she gave her mother a very lighthearted version of what had happened, and somehow managed to make it sound like nothing more serious than a prank that had gone wrong. And she didn't mention Jareth at all, she was terrified that just the mention of his name would unlock all the memories that she'd deliberately stuffed away to the very back of her mind, tear her apart all over again and send her crumbling into tiny pieces.

Calming down now that she knew her daughter was safe, her mother began to chatter on in her usual vague, charming way, and Sophie just listened to her well-loved voice and felt a sense of peace stealing over her. Promising to go and visit them for a few days as soon as she possibly could, she at last reluctantly put down the receiver and picked up the mug of coffee Kate had just brought in.

After one mouthful, she nearly choked.

'There's more brandy than coffee in this!'

'Of course there is,' agreed Kate. 'You want to feel better, don't you? Now drink it up, then we'll have our chat. By the time we've finished, I bet you'll be pleased you didn't get married.'

Sophie's velvet brown eyes instantly clouded over, and her new-found sense of peace swiftly vanished.

'But I did.'

'Did what?' enquired Kate with sudden suspicion.

'I did get married.'

There was a long silence.

'But not to David?' asked Kate delicately at last.

Sophie shook her head.

'Then who did you marry, Sophie?'

'You wouldn't know him.'

'Tell me his name,' insisted Kate firmly. 'I know lots of people, I might have run into him at some time.'

'Jareth Kingsley.'

Even now, it gave Sophie a curious twinge of pleasure

to say his name; she savoured each syllable as it slipped off her tongue.

Kate was frowning.

'Jareth Kingsley,' she mused. 'Jareth Kingsley—I'm sure that name rings a bell. But I don't think I've ever met him. Hang on a sec.' She picked up a newspaper that was lying on the table and began leafing through the back pages.

Sophie frowned.

'What on earth are you looking for?'

'I've been going out with a stockbroker for the last couple of weeks,' Kate explained, still flicking through the pages of the paper. 'He's absolutely gorgeous, I'm mad about him, so ever since I met him I've been reading all the financial pages. That way, I can make an intelligent remark now and then when he starts talking about his work. If I've seen this Jareth Kingsley's name recently, then that's where it's got to be. I haven't read anything else since I met Richard—which shows how hopelessly besotted I am! Ah,' she pounced, 'here it is.'

Sophie almost grabbed the paper from her, her gaze tore along the headline.

'Kingsley Electronics on the brink?' it read. There followed an article which, although short on facts, insinuated that the company was in deep financial trouble, perhaps only days away from being declared bankrupt.

'What's a "cash flow problem"?' asked Sophie anxiously.

'Not enough money to meet the bills,' replied Kate succinctly.

Sophie chucked the paper to one side, reached for the phone, and dialled the operator with hands that were shaking badly, despite the brandy.

'Would you give me the number for Kingsley

Electronics, please?' she asked, when the operator finally answered, then she tapped her fingers impatiently on the table as she waited for the information.

'But if you're married to Jareth Kingsley, don't you already know the number?' asked Kate with a small frown.

'It wasn't that kind of marriage,' answered Sophie tightly.

Kate began to look slightly alarmed.

'Then what kind was it?' she queried tentatively.

'The kind that only lasted four days,' came Sophie's brief reply, then the operator was giving her the number and she scribbled it down, then began to re-dial slightly frantically.

Eventually she got through to a cool voice who informed her that Mr Kingsley wasn't in his office at the moment.

'Is that Mr Kingsley's secretary?' demanded Sophie.

'Yes, it is.'

'Then would you please give me his home address?'

There was a slightly shocked silence from the other end.

'I'm afraid I can't possibly do that, it's company policy——'

'Damn company policy!' exploded Sophie. 'Anyway, from what I've been reading in the papers, it doesn't look as if you're even going to have a company in a few days.' She paused, drew in a deep breath. No point in losing her temper. 'My name is Sophie Kingsley,' she went on in a much steadier voice. 'I'm a—a close relative of Jareth's. I've lost his address, though, and I want to go round there, see if there's anything I can do to help. Look, you can phone him and check that it's all right, if you like,' she added slightly desperately.

It had been a gamble, but it seemed to have clinched

it. There was a long silence, then in a disapproving voice the secretary finally gave her Jareth's address.

Sophie put down the receiver and turned to Kate.

'Would you ring for a taxi?' she begged. 'With luck, I'll just have time to bath and change before it gets here. And have you got anything decent I can wear?'

'Have a look through my wardrobe,' invited Kate. 'We're the same size, so everything should fit. Take whatever you want.' Then she hesitated. 'Sophie,' she said at last, 'are you sure you're doing the right thing? I mean, you haven't told me anything about this marriage of yours, but quite honestly I get the impression that it was all a huge mistake.'

Sophie's shoulders slumped.

'No, I don't know that I'm doing the right thing,' she admitted tiredly. 'But I've got to do it anyway. Will you book me that taxi, Kate?'

An hour later, with dusk falling, the taxi was turning into a quiet square in the heart of London.

'This is it, love,' said the driver. 'That house on the corner.'

Sophie paid him, got out, and walked nervously towards the elegant Georgian house with its wrought iron railings and immaculate façade. As she reached up to ring the bell, her finger hesitated, quivered, then moved steadily forward and firmly pressed it.

It was Jareth himself who opened the door, yet for a few seconds she didn't recognise him. Gone was the shaggy hair, the casual Arab clothes which was all she'd ever seen him wearing. Don't be stupid, she lectured herself a little angrily. Did you expect him to be wearing them in the middle of London? Yet she couldn't quite recognise this stranger in the dark, expensive suit, the silk shirt, his hair neatly trimmed and glistening with health.

Then she looked into his eyes, and almost sighed out loud with relief. *They* hadn't changed. So vividly blue, so intense, they were staring at her with a strange kind of hunger, for an instant she almost seemed to feel the heat that blazed behind them.

Then they became blank again, the fire was deliberately doused. And Jareth's voice, when he spoke, was chillingly remote.

'You've chosen a bad time to call, Sophie. What's the matter, couldn't you wait a few more days for the annulment? Are you *that* desperate to marry David? My lawyers are working on it as fast as they can, but there are one or two complications——'

She was hardly listening.

'Can I come in?' she asked rather breathlessly.

'What the hell for?' Then he gave a brief shrug. 'Oh, I suppose so. But you can't stay for long.'

She followed him into a large drawing room furnished in an unexpectedly old-fashioned style, large comfortable sofas and chairs, thick carpets, elegant lamps. Somehow she had expected something starkly modern. It was just one more interesting facet of the man.

'Do you want a drink?' he asked abruptly.

She remembered the large amount of brandy she had already drunk.

'No, thank you,' she said politely.

'Well, I need one,' growled Jareth. He poured himself a drink then, because it was rapidly growing dark outside, he drew the curtains and switched on a couple of the lamps.

When he turned to face her, the electric glare shone full on to his face and she caught her breath.

'You look tired to death!'

He shrugged irritably.

'It's not important.' He slumped down on to the sofa,

seeming too exhausted even to swallow the drink he'd poured. 'Okay, Sophie, what are you doing here? I told you, you'll get your annulment, but it's going to take time, a bit more time than I originally expected. I'm sorry about that, but it can't be helped.'

'I came because I heard about the company,' Sophie answered simply.

His eyes flickered warily.

'Come to gloat?' Then he saw her face, gave a weary sigh. 'Sorry, I didn't mean that. You've got a lot of faults, but malice isn't one of them.'

There was so much she wanted to say. It was just that she didn't know where to start, couldn't even find the right words. Then she saw his face, saw that he was so tired that nothing she said would probably make any sense anyhow. His eyes were shadowed with utter exhaution; she guessed that he'd driven himself relentlessly over the past couple of weeks, trying desperately to save his company.

She walked over to him and sat down beside him.

'When did you last sleep?' she asked quietly.

'Can't remember,' he muttered.

'Then go to sleep now. Jareth, you can't do anything while you're in this state, you look too tired to even think straight any more.'

'Can't sleep,' came his slurred confession. 'I've tried, but I just can't. It doesn't matter how damned tired I am, I *can't sleep*.'

She heard the note of desperation in his voice, and knew then what she had to do.

She looked steadily into those achingly familiar blue eyes.

'I can make you sleep,' she told him softly.

'I don't want pills,' he snapped back irritably. 'I've tried them, they just make my brain even more foggy.'

'I'm not going to give you any pills. Take off your jacket and tie, and lie back on the sofa.'

Jareth's gaze flickered in puzzlement.

'What?'

'Lie back on the sofa,' Sophie repeated patiently.

'Whatever you've got in mind, it won't work,' he warned her. 'I've tried everything.' But he obeyed her all the same, sprawled out on the large, soft sofa, his dark head resting against the cushion at one end.

She kicked off her shoes and stretched out beside him. There was plenty of room for the two of them, as long as they lay fairly close.

'What the hell are you doing?' he muttered suspiciously.

She gave him a demure smile.

'We've slept together plenty of times in the past,' she reminded him. 'I thought perhaps we ought to try it again.'

'Stop it, Sophie!' he ordered sharply. 'I'm not in the mood for games tonight.'

She looked down at him, at the dark, familiar planes of his face.

'But I think that's exactly what you need right now,' she murmured, her fingers drifting delicately down to the first button of his shirt. 'A few interesting little games to take your mind off all your problems. Do you remember how you taught me to play "forfeits", Jareth?'

For the first time his exhausted mind realised what she was about to do; she saw all his defences fly into place, as if he were determined to resist this assault on his tired senses.

'No, Sophie,' he said, almost grimly. 'I won't allow it.'

Her fingers slid down to the second button, released

it, crept under the fine material to find the warm, supple skin underneath.

'I don't remember telling you that you were being given a choice,' she said a little huskily.

Inside, she was shaking, but her hands were perfectly steady as they slid across the rigidly tense muscles, coaxing them into the first stages of relaxation.

The vivid blue gaze abruptly darkened a shade, and she sensed a faint weakening of that iron self-control.

'No, Sophie,' Jareth ordered again, but this time there was less conviction in his voice, he made no effort to push her hands away. Heart thumping so fast that she could hardly breathe now, she felt his own hands involuntarily move, grip her waist and pull her down, keeping her clasped tight against him.

'You're like a honey-trap, all sweetness,' he muttered thickly. 'I promised myself I'd never let this happen again, but I'm so damned tired I don't know what I'm doing, I don't even know if this is for real.'

Sophie bent her head, leaving a trail of butterfly-light kisses against the warm skin at the base of his throat; she rubbed her cheek luxuriously against the crisp hair of his chest before resting her face against his breastbone, where she could hear the heavy, erratic thudding of his heart.

'Did that feel real?' she asked a little tremulously.

Jareth didn't answer, his mouth was already busy exploring every inch of her soft skin that it could reach. When he encountered the rough edge of her dress, he gave a small grunt of frustration and flipped her over on to her back. She heard her dress tear, but didn't care, she'd buy Kate another one to replace it, half a dozen. Nothing was of any consequence any more, nothing except the touch of Jareth's hands and mouth on her hot, fevered body, moving swiftly, almost roughly, demanding everything she had to give, and more.

A sleeping tiger, that was how she had once described his dormant sexuality to herself. And now she had deliberately prodded that tiger into life, forgetting what a fiercely ruthless animal it was, seizing what it wanted, showing no mercy. She ought to be terrified—but she wasn't. Her body purred shamelessly under his sensual assault, breasts swollen and aching under the moist touch of his tongue, stomach muscles contracting wildly as his clever hands swept down to claim what was his.

Slick skin touched slick skin, fanned wave after wave of heat, then his mouth was on hers, burning its brand on to her bruised lips, marking her for life.

'You're mine, you were always mine, right from the very beginning,' he told her hoarsely, and as if to emphasise his right to claim her, he rolled over on top of her, she was trapped by the crushing weight of his body, the full force of his desire pressing hard against her own quivering flesh.

'Say it,' he ordered roughly. 'Say it!'

The blue gaze pinned her to the sofa more effectively than the strength of his powerful limbs, their blazing light was a dazzling revelation.

'I'm yours,' Sophie whispered weakly, knowing that it was true, that she could never, ever belong to anyone else, even if he threw her out in the morning and refused to see her again.

Her murmured confession seemed to rouse him to new depths of desire, the flush across his cheekbones darkened, his breathing was as wild as her own.

'It's been years since anyone's done this to me,' he muttered, his hands moving almost convulsively across the throbbing swell of her breasts, 'but I can't wait for you any longer, Sophie, I can't——'

There was no time even to strip off the last of their

clothes; Sophie could feel the explosive force building and building inside him to uncontrollable levels. Then he was crushing her, forcing himself into her, shuddering with the helpless intensity of his need. A sharp flare of pain surprised her, then it was gone, forgotten, and her own body was moving to match his, locked into its own sweetly pagan rhythm, the tempo building and rising, swirling up and up until she could hear her own voice crying out, then Jareth was groaning too with the fierceness of his pleasure as the world exploded into a thousand tiny fragments of shimmering delight.

Seconds later, he was asleep. His body still hot and damp and heavy against hers, he was swallowed up by the total exhaustion that had dogged him for days. Locked tight against him, Sophie cradled his dark head against her breast, feeling like the embodiment of every female since Eve had first left the Garden of Eden. Inside her, she was aware of a glorious sense of exultation, an inner fire that burnt with a bright incandescence, like a flame in the darkness. For a long time, she fought off her own tiredness, wanting to hold on to every moment of this unbearably sweet intimacy. Then, at last, her eyes dropped shut and she too fell asleep.

When she woke up again, the first glow of early morning light was filtering through the curtains and Jareth was lying beside her, propped up on one elbow, studying her face.

'Have I grown two noses during the night?' she teased lightly as he continued with his absorbed inspection of her features.

'No, but you've grown more beautiful,' he answered with a touch of wonderment. 'I really didn't think it was possible, but you have.'

'And what do you think could have caused this

phenomenon?' she asked gravely.

'I've no idea,' he replied, gently stroking her cheek with one finger. 'Something must have happened since you walked through that door last night.'

Sophie allowed her gaze to grow wide and innocent.

'I don't *remember* anything startling happening,' she mused thoughtfully.

'Then perhaps you need a little something to jog your memory——'

Jareth's hand moved so swiftly that she had no time to prepare for what was coming; then a delicious echo of pleasure was curling through her body, she released a tiny moan of need as his hand moved away again, deliberately teasing now, causing those tiny flutters to swirl provocatively through her nerve-ends, leaving her writhing restlessly under his touch.

Then he paused, looked down at her with new intensity.

'I'll never let you go, not now,' he said in a voice that wasn't entirely steady. 'You know that, don't you? I know you love David, but you'll just have to forget about him, I'll *make* you forget about him.'

There was a sudden note of almost raw pain in his voice. She couldn't bear to hear it, and quickly put up one hand to soothe away the tiny lines that had appeared at the corners of his mouth.

'I don't love David,' she told him almost shyly. 'I was very fond of him and I admired him tremendously, but I never did love him, I realise that now. It was just—well, I had nothing to compare it with before, so I got mixed up, and thought affection and love were the same thing. Then I fell in love with you and I realised just what a mistake I'd made about David, only I thought it was too late, because I'd already promised to marry him——'

'Say that again!' Jareth interrupted tersely.

She blinked.

'Say what?'

'That part about falling in love with me.'

She stared up at him slightly indignantly.

'But you must *know* that I love you. Good heavens,' she went on, blushing furiously, 'you don't think that—well, last night—that I'd behave like that with just *anyone*, do you?'

'Then say it,' he ordered.

Sophie's tongue flickered a little nervously across her lips.

'I love you,' she said in a small voice.

'Again. But louder.'

'I love you.'

The vivid blue eyes began to dance with amusement.

'Once more!' he commanded.

'I love you!'

'And I love you,' he answered her, only in a much gentler tone this time.

'You do?'

'Of course,' he said with a touch of impatience. 'You don't think that *I'd* behave like I did last night with just anyone, do you? For heaven's sake, I'm thirty-five years old, Sophie, I learnt all the lessons of self-control by the time I was in my early twenties. I didn't think anyone could make me forget them, whip up such a storm in my blood that I'd go nearly out of my head with wanting just one small girl with apricot hair.' He hesitated for a moment, then went on, 'Walking away from you that day in the desert, leaving you there with David, was the hardest thing I'd ever done in my entire life. I wanted to grab you, run off with you, *force* you to love me.'

'But—it was just a marriage of convenience,' she stuttered.

He smiled a trifle grimly.

'I knew from that moment I first asked you to marry me that I wanted it to be for real. But you kept insisting you were in love with David, so I knew I had to clear out of your life, let you have the man you really wanted, even though it nearly killed me.'

'The man I wanted was you,' Sophie confessed quietly.

Jareth bent his head to kiss her again, then gave a small groan.

'It's getting late. All I want to do is lie here and make love to you, but I've got to get to the office. Unless I can raise a very large sum of cash by the end of today, Kingsley Electronics is going to go under.'

Reluctantly he got up and drew back the curtains, letting in a flood of daylight. Then he came back to stand by the sofa, running his fingers frustratedly through his dark, tangled hair as he stared down at her.

'I read in the papers something about a cash flow problem,' Sophie said, her eyes becoming serious. 'Is it very bad?'

'Bad enough,' he confirmed. 'Brian Peters, the man I left in charge while I was away, made a few bad errors of judgement concerning finance. Then we've had production difficulties with a few of our new gadgets, they won't be in the shops for some weeks yet, and in the meantime production costs are mounting up without bringing in anything in return. The company's basically sound. If we can hang on for just a couple more months, we'll be fine. What I need is a large loan to tide me over, meet the everyday expenses until the company's on a financially sound footing again.'

'Have you managed to get the loan?'

'Only part of it,' he told her rather tensely. 'I've got roughly twenty-four hours to raise the rest or that's it, the company will go under. And I've already knocked

myself out trying to raise the rest of the loan, I just don't
know who else I can approach.'

Sophie's delicate brows drew together thoughtfully.
'How much do you need?'

'About two hundred and fifty thousand.' He lifted his
shoulders in a helpless shrug. 'Doesn't sound much if
you say it quickly, does it?' he added humourlessly.

'I could lend you that much,' she said.

There was a moment of stunned silence.

'Sophie, don't tease me,' he said a little sharply at last,
'not about this.'

She stared at him solemnly.

'I'm not teasing,' she assured him. 'I know you're
going to find this a little embarrassing, but the fact is—
well, you've married an heiress. An uncle of mine spent
his whole life playing around with stocks and shares. He
had a real flair for picking the right ones, buying at rock
bottom prices and watching them shoot up. And when
he died, he left the lot to me.' She smiled sheepishly. 'I
really am worth an awful lot of money.'

Jareth shook his head in astonishment.

'How many more surprises are you going to spring on
me, Sophie?' Then his face became more set. 'But I'm
not going to take a penny of your money,' he warned
her.

She shook her head in exasperation. Male pride! But
she'd known all along he'd raise this objection, and she
had already thought of a way round it.

'I'm not offering to give it to you, Jareth, I said I'd
lend it to you. I'd expect current interest rates on the
loan, and it'll all be done legally, with the proper papers
drawn up.' She smiled with some satisfaction. 'I think
Uncle Harold would be rather proud of me. Your
company seemes like a very sound investment and I

should get a good return on my money. Your company *is* sound, isn't it?'

'As a rock,' he said at once, a little indignantly. 'Once we get over this bad patch, profits will soar, we've got some electronic gadgets coming out that'll sweep the market.'

'Oh, good,' she said with some satisfaction. 'Then it looks like the perfect place to invest my money.' As Jareth still wavered, she went on in a thoughtful tone, 'If you agree to the loan, you won't have to go chasing off in search of someone else to lend it to you, will you? And we'll have the rest of the day to ourselves.'

Her eyes sparkled at him invitingly, but he still hesitated. Then, to her relief, she saw his mouth relax.

'All right, I'll accept your offer,' he told her. 'But only on one condition.'

'What's that?' she asked a little suspiciously.

'That you come and work for the company,' he replied promptly. As she stared at him in amazement, he went on persuasively, 'I need someone like you to promote sales of our new products, Sophie. You've got a good brain, you're quick-witted, I've got a feeling in my guts that you'd be damned good at selling.'

She blinked.

'But I don't know the first thing about electronics,' she protested.

'I'll teach you,' he responded immediately. His mouth curved into a teasing smile. 'I'm a good teacher, remember?' As she blushed, he grinned, then went on, 'Seriously, Sophie, will you have a shot at it? At least, for a few months, until the company's on its feet? I think you'll enjoy it, it'll be a challenge, something you can really get your teeth into. And if later on you want to have kids, then you can either pack it in or carry on part-time, whichever you want.'

Her eyes already glowing with interest, Sophie nodded vigorously.

'I'd like to have a shot at it, I really would,' she said, a little breathlessly. 'When can I start?'

One dark eyebrow lifted expressively.

'Not for the next few hours,' Jareth told her a little huskily.

She stared up at him blankly for a couple of seconds; then realisation dawned and she stretched sensually, batting her long eyelashes at him.

'Well, I suppose it's all right, we *are* married,' she said demurely.

His hand had already begun to play gentle, delicious games with her taut nipples, but to her surprise he suddenly drew back.

'Actually, there's something I ought to have mentioned to you before,' he said in a faintly apologetic tone. 'Only there wasn't a lot of opportunity for conversation last night.'

'What should you have mentioned?' asked Sophie slightly suspiciously.

'Well——' He hesitated, then gave a wry shrug. 'It rather looks as if we might not be married at all.'

'What?' she yelped.

'Remember that I told you last night that there were some complications about the annulment?'

Still stunned, she nodded blankly.

'No one seems to have any record of a Father Donoghue working in that part of the Sahara,' Jareth went on. 'It's starting to look as if the good Father might have set himself up as a free-lance representative of the church.'

Sophie stared at him in dismay.

'You mean he wasn't authorised to marry us?'

'The solicitors are still checking, but it looks as if it might turn out that way. And even if they do find he's legitimate, there's still the fact that you got married without having the proper papers. The chances of our marriage being valid are pretty slim.' And while she was still unhappily contemplating exactly what that meant, he went on more gently, 'So I'm afraid we're going to have to get married all over again, just to make sure it's perfectly legal.'

Sophie blinked dazedly.

'Married?' she echoed.

'Church, vicar, bridesmaids, hordes of relations and a three-tier wedding cake,' he agreed solemnly. 'Do you think you can stand it?'

Her face absolutely radiant, all she could do was nod jerkily.

'And now that's settled,' Jareth went on in a suddenly changed voice, 'there are one or two other important matters to be taken care of. Now, where were we when we were interrupted?'

As he reached for her, she melted into his arms, still smiling happily. Then her smile faltered slightly, and for a moment she resisted him.

'But, Jareth, if we're not married——' she began with a slight frown.

'Just this once, my lady,' he coaxed her, and the breath sighed lightly in her throat. She loved this man, she wanted him, she couldn't resist the delicately sensual touch of his fingers as he slowly, lovingly caressed her into melting delight.

'And perhaps just once more,' he murmured a little later as she curled up against the lean, strong body she adored, feeling his leaping response to her innocent teasing.

Then they slept in each other's arms as the sun filtered through the windows, bathing their bodies in its clear golden light.

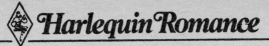

Harlequin Romance

Coming Next Month

2869 CARPENTARIA MOON Kerry Allyne
Photographer Eden arrives to be tourist director at an Australian
cattle station, asked by Alick, a friend, but finds the station is
owned by his older brother who regards her as the latest girlfriend
Alick is trying to dump!

2870 WINNER TAKE ALL Kate Denton
When a campaign manager recommends that her boss, a Louisiana
congressman, find a wife to dispel his playboy reputation, she
never thinks she'll be the one tying the knot!

2871 FORCE FIELD Jane Donnelly
For a young amateur actress, playing Rosalind in an open-air
production in Cornwall is enjoyable. But being emotionally torn
between the estate owner's two sons, a sculptor and an artist, is
distressing—until real love, as usual, settles the matter.

2872 THE EAGLE AND THE SUN Dana James
Jewelry designer Cass Elliott expects to enjoy a working holiday
until her boss's son unexpectedly accompanies her and their arrival
in Mexico proves untimely. She's excited by the instant rapport
between herself and their Mexican host, then she learns that Miguel
is already engaged....

2873 SHADOW FALL Rowan Kirby
Brought together by a young girl needing strong emotional
support, a London schoolteacher and the pupil's widowed father
fall in love. Then she learns of her resemblance to his deceased wife
and can't help wondering if she's just a substitute.

2874 OFF WITH THE OLD LOVE Betty Neels
All of Rachel's troubles about being engaged to a TV producer
who doesn't understand her nursing job and expects her to drop
everything for his fashionable social life are confided to the
comfortable Dutch surgeon, Radmer. Then, surprisingly, she finds
Radmer is the man she loves!

Available in November wherever paperback books are sold, or
through Harlequin Reader Service.

In the U.S.
901 Fuhrmann Blvd.
P.O. Box 1397
Buffalo, N.Y. 14240-1397

In Canada
P.O. Box 603
Fort Erie, Ontario
L2A 5X3

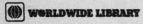

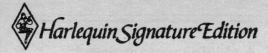

Penny Jordan

Stronger Than Yearning

He was the man of her dreams!

The same dark hair, the same mocking eyes; it was as if the Regency rake of the portrait, the seducer of Jenna's dream, had come to life. Jenna, believing the last of the Deverils dead, was determined to buy the great old Yorkshire Hall—to claim it for her daughter, Lucy, and put to rest some of the painful memories of Lucy's birth. She had no way of knowing that a direct descendant of the black sheep Deveril even existed—or that James Allingham and his own powerful yearnings would disrupt her plan entirely.

Penny Jordan's first Harlequin Signature Edition *Love's Choices* was an outstanding success. Penny Jordan has written more than 40 best-selling titles—more than 4 million copies sold.

Now, be sure to buy her latest bestseller, *Stronger Than Yearning*. Available wherever paperbacks are sold—in October.

An enticing
new historical romance!

Spring
Will Come
SHERRY DeBORDE

It was 1852, and the steamy South was in its last hours of
gentility. Camille Braxton Beaufort went searching for the
one man she knew she could trust, and under his protection had her first lesson in love....

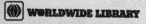